Pocket Companion: A Tavern Guide

WISDOM SAVE
—— M E D I A ——

Introduction

Welcome to the Pocket Companion, a book produced by Wis Save Media. We are a group of Tabletop Gaming geeks who felt there were too many expensive products that made Tabletop Gaming inaccessible to a lot of people.

That's a huge shame, so we wanted to produce products to allow both experienced and new gamers to get involved.

We ran a short crowdfunding round in 2017 in the hope of bringing together the gaming community to create a crowdsourced guide to taverns. To say that the project was a success would be an understatement, with hundreds of people from around the world contributing their taverns and characters to produce a mammoth 150-page A4 book.

As a result, this book was born. Pulling together some of the best taverns and characters from the Tavern Companion, along with plot hooks, roll tables and reference guides in a pocket-sized format. It provides a one-stop shop for seasoned adventurers, as well as those looking to embark on their first quest.

We want to say a massive thank you to all that have supported us on our journey, your passion and creativity have inspired us endlessly, and we hope you enjoy the result.

All our thanks,
The Wisdom Save Media Team

Contents

Plot

Hooks

'A Troubling Situation'

After settling in for a night of drinking and revelry, a
somewhat flustered looking dwarf makes his way to the bar.
A wave of disgruntled patrons and disturbed
furniture lies in his wake as the rain-soaked figure climbs a
bar stall to meet the bar tender's eye.

A few people's eyes are drawn to the commotion, but the
noise of the other patrons makes it difficult to hear the conversation between the nervous looking fellow and the cheery
barkeep. At some point during their exchange, the barman
becomes concerned and cautiously hands the dwarf a room
key in exchange for far more coin than it was worth. The
dwarf darts off to the rooms above creating yet another path
of chaos and disruption.

Meanwhile, the barkeep shakes off his fearful look and returns
to his duties, quickly inserting himself into another conversation at the bar. His booming laughter returns, lending itself to
the ambience of this peaceful tavern.

The following morning the dwarf is found dead in his room.
How did it happen? Was he trying to outrun a curse? Did
he fall prey to a malicious spell? Or was it a case of pure,
cold-blooded murder?

The local law enforcement might chalk this up as
another unsolved murder, but who's to say it will not happen
again?

'Delayed Festivities'

The tavern is crowded and noisy, which is not unusual for a tavern. But, it's difficult to open the door, and the noise doesn't sound good. Tied to the rafters over the dark ale-stained bar banners announce today's beer festival, hanging gleefully above a panic-stricken barkeep. Over the noise of impatient patrons, the bartender attempts once again to make an announcement. He begins by apologising humbly for the late arrival of the master brewer. He assures his disgruntled audience that the master brewer's arrival is imminent; as is the arrival of the finest ales the land has to offer.

Mumblings of discontent begin as the barkeep raises his voice a final time. As though it were his prized possession, the bartender walks over to a large cask and places a loving arm over it. He announces that the cask was a gift from the master brewer the last time he travelled to the tavern. With the most pained look he can muster, the barkeep declares that he will open the cask and the patrons will have their first drink for free as thanks for their patience. Cups begin to be filled, and the mood of the room increases dramatically.

A quiet conversation with the barkeep reveals that the master brewer was expected hours ago. Was he simply late? Or has he been held up by bandits? Or worse? Maybe he'll hire some people that could look into this for him.

'A Warm Reception'

Taverns and inns tend to be a source of revelry and fun, but this tavern more so. Since your arrival, the staff and its patrons have been exceptionally welcoming. News of your good deeds and heroism seems to have sparked something within them that has given them cause for celebration.

The excellent ale casks have been tapped, a banquet is being prepared, and the best bards in town are tuning their instruments in preparation for a night of feasting and entertainment. It is in your honour that they wish to dine and dance, and have offered to provide all this for nothing. Your room is paid for, your drink is free, and the food is complimentary. Every face you meet is friendly and no matter whom you talk to – be it staff or patron – they can't do enough for you. They cater to your every desire and ensure every whim is met. It's a perfect night. Almost too perfect.

The night never seems to end, food is brought out in endless courses, another follows every actor's piece of music, and the casks appear to be bottomless.

Though they don't seem to mind if you retire to your room, but diversion and temptation meet any attempts to leave the establishment. If that doesn't work, they might resort to physical persuasion. If they manage to keep you for an overnight stay, you might wake up to find yourself in a locked cage at the mercy of the creatures that tricked you into staying here.

'Daylight Robbery'

Inside the grubby tavern its patrons sit quietly in patient anticipation. All that can be heard is hushed conversation as these bandits lie in wait for their prey. They used to utilise their skills on the roads, taking advantage of the thriving trade route nearby, but the caravan owners started hiring sellswords and would-be adventurers to protect their cargo. With their numbers at an all-time low, their leader decided to switch tactics. After chasing off a local tavern owner, the bandit leader swapped his scale mail for an apron and began waiting for the loot to walk straight in.

With their guard down and their wits dulled by ale, it was easy pickings. They had even managed to boost their numbers by recruiting some morally questionable hirelings during this prosperous time. Not every caravan would be ransacked or raided however - that would be bad for business. He even provided attentive service to his unsuspecting patrons from time-to-time. That's not to say they left with all their wares and goods, but they weren't emptied and burned like some more unfortunate targets.

So there they sit, making more coin than they ever had before while enjoying the comforts of staying in a tavern to boot. But who knows? Maybe their next victims will possess more skill and cunning than previous ones.

The Tavern Guide

Introduction

Each entry within the Tavern Guide section of the book aims to provide you with the information you need to improvise and play out a fulfilling tavern visit. The Tavern Guide is split into sections so you can narrow down the type of tavern you require. For example, if your players are travelling through an urban environment, you may want to pick something from the Cities and Towns chapter, but there's no reason why you couldn't choose one at random!

At the top of each tavern entry, you will find the name of the tavern with a rating underneath. The rating is measured out of five, and the more casks a tavern has earned, the better the service your players can expect. This takes into consideration:

Customer Service	Comfort
Quality of Produce	Range of services available
Décor	Overall customer satisfaction

Consider the impact of cost on the tavern's rating. If you are using a five-cask tavern, have the owners raised the prices with their newfound customer base? Or is their rating as a result of being the cheapest? If you're using a one-cask tavern are the owners charging too much, and so no one goes there? Or are the prices incredibly low but only because everything from the ale to the beds are awful?

Under the title of the tavern entry, you will find icons that represent the various services available to patrons of the tavern. This is by no means an extensive or restrictive list but can be used as a quick reference guide to confirm what they have to offer.

Food

Many establishments offer food and other edible goods to their patrons. Taverns with this icon, however, have shown a degree of finesse with their food. These establishments not only have a working kitchen and likely a full-time chef, but they also have a menu and serving staff capable of greeting, seating and feeding the patrons.

Stables

Stables are often found attached to the tavern proper or at least nearby, as some establishments aim to please all who visit – including the patron's trusty steed. Taverns with this icon have the facilities to care for and house the player's horses wagons for a fee, and some of the larger ones may even be able to accommodate carts and wagons. The proprietors may also allow patrons to pay a small fee to sleep in the hay for a night instead of parting with substantial sums of coin for a room. Taverns without this symbol may still be able to accommodate horses and other beasts of burden, although this is less likely in densely populated areas. These taverns will sometimes have the odd hitching post or two, and the feed and water necessary, but it's just not quite the same as an actual stable.

Rooms

Besides the undeniable attraction to these places, there is sometimes the promise of a safe and cosy bed to rest one's head. Taverns with this icon are capable of housing many guests and have an array of room options available to cater to the masses. The standards of these rooms, however, can vary greatly.

Merchants

As they tend to provide everything the weary traveller may need, some taverns hold a selection of items to trade for coin. Taverns with this icon have either a barkeep with the capability to trade goods for coin or have dedicated merchants that operate within or around the tavern. The stock will vary from tavern to tavern, and the goods may not always be physical items, many barkeeps made their fortune by dealing in secrets and rumours.

Establishments lacking a merchant icon show that it is either not possible to purchase equipment and supplies, or indicate there is not a reliable source of trade within the tavern. It is likely when travelling from place to place that you might find a travelling merchant within a tavern, but the taverns lacking this symbol suggest you cannot rely on passing traders to be there.

Blacksmith

A rare sight to behold, but there's no sweeter relief than returning from a gruelling fight to find a blacksmith attached to or near a tavern. The icon suggests that the tavern can also provide services such as armour repair and weapon sharpening. The 'smithy' may also have the have the stock available to give the patrons newer equipment or perhaps commission some work to be done. In more populated areas, passing trade is managed in the usual fashion, but patrons of the tavern tend to receive discounts on smithing services. Taverns lacking this symbol do not have access to a working forge, though the staff may have some experience in the smithing arts. In any case, most proprietors will be able to point players in the right direction.

Entertainment

If the tavern has this symbol it suggests it boasts some form of in-house entertainment available on most occasions, be it a resident bard or a barkeep with a particular talent for storytelling. It is important to note that entertainment is a somewhat vague term, as what people may consider being entertaining is wholly influenced by the location of the tavern and the culture of those around it. It is possible that these taverns have the space available for ad hoc performances, or perhaps they recently lost their resident bard. In any case, many can find their entertainment within a house of ale.

Bar Staff and Patrons

Taverns are there to provide services to patrons. Notice that I did not specify that it is their sole purpose? To offer a specific service, the tavern needs staff, and similarly, the tavern needs patrons in order to make money. Alongside the

tavern information, there are some non-playable characters to give you the perfect people to drop into any situation to interact with your player characters. The bar-staff and patrons are arranged to provide you with their names, their race, and their occupation. The basic information included gives you an idea of their appearance, and below that is a list of attributes that give you an insight into their personality.

Cities and
Towns

Cities and towns, large and small, have one thing in common. They are bursting with establishments that cater to the thirsty and the weary. There is something about thick walls and city guards that make people go a little crazier than they would in the wilderness. Maybe it's a shared delusion of safety, but we can assure you there are as many dangers within the walls as there are monsters that lurk outside them.

Barrel Baron Tavern

Description
A simple looking timber framed tavern stands before you surrounded by empty barrels. From the smell, they appear to have been full of ale. The noise of revelry and laughter fills your ears as you enter the roaring atmosphere of the Barrel Baron Tavern. The bar area is packed and there is no sign of an empty chair in sight. The only thing louder than the patrons is the laughter and booming voice of the barrel baron himself, Lord Kegmen.

A Bit O' History
Opened by the self-titled 'Lord' Kegman, he spent his entire family's fortune filling this old house with barrels of beer.

The tavern is well known for cheap ale, cheap food, and drunk bards. Some would say he was a foolish man but the Barrel Baron now owns one of the largest houses in the city. A fool he may be, but a rich fool at that.

Reviews
Bryn Lampwood 4/5
"Best beer in town! And plenty of it!"

Kasandra Tylmarsh 3/5
"It's always so busy! Never a seat to enjoy your drink in peace, though, it is cheap, I wonder how he can afford to sell it so cheap?"

Staff and Patrons of the Barrel Baron Tavern
Dave (High elf: Wizard)
Dave is a 237-year-old, standing just a little shorter then
Kriv, and has six inches of straight blond hair. He dresses
in dark-blue robes, dark-brown leather boots and travelling
pants. His robes have the sigil of the Wardens stitched into
the right shoulder. As a Warden, Dave is dedicated to
studying, learning, and collecting ancient artefacts.

Likes: Elven wine, history Dislikes: Barbarians, gods & goddesses, religious intuitions Wants: To learn, to discover lost secrets	Fears: That the gods and goddesses will bring war Flaws: Arrogant, aloft, thinks he is right about everything

Kriv (Half dragon: Fighter)
Kriv is a 35-year-old Half-Dragon, standing tallest of the
three companions, with tarnished silver scales. Kriv has a long
scar running down the left side of his face, which was caused
by a hellhound. A veteran of several conflicts at a young age,
Kriv rose to the rank of Captain due to his leadership ability.

Likes: Drinks, fights, money Dislikes: Uptight folks Wants: To be known	Fears: Being forgotten Flaws: Quick to anger, likes to drink a little too much

Dahal (Half demon: Rogue)
Dahal is 33 years old, a little shorter than his companions,
and keeps his slivery hair cut short, often hidden under some
headgear. Dahal often plays with one of his hidden daggers
whenever he is bored, nervous or stressed.

Likes: Gold, money, friends Dislikes: Uptight folks Wants: Gold, money	Fears: Imprisonment Flaws: Very sarcastic, does not like to make plans

Black Coin Lounge

Description

This two-story building looks well maintained from the outside. The double doors bear a large carving of a gold coin, painted jet black with gold accents. No windows can be found inside, and Blazicurses and shouts of delight can be heard as patrons move from the bar to the gambling tables. A stage in the back rotates through travelling bards and local showgirls, and you'll notice a gambling-free seating area in the front.

A Bit O' History

Established only a few months ago by a local gambling addict who won big, this tavern has already gained enormous popularity for its promoted gambling. Dice games and card games are the most favourable, but patrons can usually find someone willing to bet on anything. The food is nothing special, and the entertainment often depends on who's in town, but most patrons don't mind these shortcomings.

Reviews

Derrek Aaronson 4/5
"May just be lucky, but I've come out ahead more often than not at the coin."

Niramor Brightleaf 1/5
"If you want anything other than gambling, don't visit. Poor food, crowded rooms, and the seating area doesn't allow for conversation. I left after one drink, and won't be returning."

Blazing Bear Inn

Description

Nestled between half collapsed buildings, the only thing that draws attention to the Inn is the noise of its patrons. Only then do you notice the big sign of a burning, roaring bear. The inside is a mess of many different styles; with finely carved chairs standing next to tables of bone. The drink selection is no different; you can order everything from the cheapest beer and ale to expensive, exotic wines and liquors.

A Bit O' History

The Inn seemed to appear out of nowhere and gain popularity quickly. It was founded by a group of adventurers, looking to find a relaxing space to return to and a place to share their stories. Anyone who can tell a good story about themselves is welcome to add their personal touch to the Inn, and people travel from far away to add a trophy or a piece of furniture to the ever-growing collection of legends.

Reviews

Arlech Admundsen 5/5

"Best place I've been in a long time. It has nothing to do with that I'm the head of entertainment. Nothing. Come visit, it's great. I accept tips."

Advena Silvis 3/5

"It has a kind of charm to it, I suppose. Still, would it hurt to clean up more and invest in better food? I need my food!"

Staff and Patrons of the Blazing Bear Inn

Rue (High-Elf: Bartender/ Detective)
Rue is rarely noticed. Her appearance, and the way she acts, does not make her memorable. Her hair is black, her skin is lightly tanned and her eyes dark. Rue is often dressed in dark clothes, hiding leather armour beneath it, so she freely can move around without looking suspicious.

Likes: Looting, stealing Dislikes: Sharing secrets, making people upset Wants: Lots of gold	Fears: Dragons, fire Flaws: Only follows laws if people are watching

Aster Fairwyck (Halfling: Bouncer)
From a distance she looks every bit the noble she is but, as you get closer, you quickly realise she is a warrior at heart. She carries herself with grace but also determination. Her hair is golden, her eyes brown and her skin fair. She often wears armour, but can also be seen in beautiful dresses.

Likes: Money, bashing things Dislikes: Bears, people who see her as weak Wants: Her father's recognition	Fears: Having to be idle Flaws: He never back down from a fight

Glim Moonglow Barnor (Gnome: Healer)
Even though he always looks irritated this gnome is happy to help. His hair is almost white and his skin shows that he has spent many hours in the sun. His eyes are green, but they seem to change shade with the seasons.

Likes: Keeping promises Dislikes: Goblins, orcs, undead Wants: To be free	Fears: Losing family Flaws: Money does not make sense to me

Bottle and Barrel

Description
From the outside it looks well maintained, clean and cheerful, standing three stories tall. Bricks and sandstone pillars make up most of the building's outer structure. The front door is metal and looks heavily used, and the windows are all stained glass of various colours. Inside, tree logs support the upper floors and large candles attached to them light the big common/eating room, as well as the various hallways and rooms. The main common room boasts a long L-shaped bar.

A Bit O' History
The Bottle and Barrel was founded in what used to be wilderness, and was established by a former adventuring/mercenary company known for prominent achievements 30-50 years ago. The adventurers and their sons still run the tavern today. The Bottle and Barrel, and the area around it, has grown over the years partly due to the popularity of the adventurers that founded the tavern.

Reviews
Hozz Tusk 2/5
"Too clean. The bartender is always angry when the tavern is dirty. I work in fields. Beer is good though."

John Buck 5/5
"I love this place! All the people are nice, especially our waitress. The drinks are great. Did I mention the waitress...?"

The Cloak

Description
The tavern is a simple two-story building with two outbuildings. When you enter the tavern, the bar is located in the centre of the room. Around the bar, you will find small tables and chairs neatly arranged to give each table a little privacy. At the back of the room are two doors. The first leads to the kitchen and then on to the tavern keeper's rooms. The second door leads to the upper floor where you will find five guest rooms. There are also two outbuildings; one is a simple stable, the other is a storage shed.

A Bit O' History
The Cloak was opened by a Rasser, a retired adventurer who spent many years travelling with a famous band of adventurers, the Crimson Cloaks. Looking to settle down, he took his share of the loot and opened the Cloak. On slow nights Rasser entertains his guest by recounting the many adventures of the Crimson Cloaks. Some say that Rasser has not entirely given up his old life and still has contacts among the Crimson Cloaks, as well as with specific less reputable figures.

Reviews
Aegmund Falka 2/5
"A nice enough place but the brews are nothing like I'm used to. I prefer a cheeky little number."

The Copper Coin

Description

The smell of cooked meat hits you first as the cheer of a crowd fills your ears. A group of bards play to a lively crowd down one end of this enormous room. A dark oak bar runs along the entire wall, manned by well over a dozen men and dwarves. Barrels fill the walls behind the bar up to the gallery that runs around the whole circumference of the tavern. A glorious fire pit sits in the centre with fresh meat and sausages cooking on spits.

A Bit O' History

The busy commercial district is a hubbub of traders, smiths, cutthroats and sailors. The snow falls thick most of the year in these northern towns, but the cold is never felt in The Copper Coin. A popular joint in the north, and a great place to meet all manner of traders and shop owners, it's always been a traveller's inn and grew along with the city as it expanded from being a small town. Less a place for secrets and rumours, it's more suited for the road worn adventurer as soft beds are also available in the loft.

Reviews

Stavos Grayson 5/5

"Local talent, local flavour and some of the best local girls I've ever seen."

Drunken Dwarf

Description
As you close the heavy oaken door behind you the noise from the street immediately stops, replaced by the low murmur of conversations from the patrons. The dimly lit space is finished with dark wood, with sconces on the walls. There are four booths along the left-hand wall, four small round tables occupying the centre of the space, and four stools against the long wooden bar. It's a place of comfort, a place to relax and a place of quiet conversation.

A Bit O' History
The Drunken Dwarf has been an established part of the local merchant community since the city's founding. It's well respected for the quality of its food and drink, and the privacy afforded its clientele. The owner, Silas Brown, has been hiding Rurik Ungart, who deals in information from a secret room behind the kitchen.

Reviews
Thorbjorn Hrungnirson 4/5
"The quality of the beer is exceeded only by that of the information which can be acquired here."

Magus Brendark 5/5
"Excellent location for a discrete conversation over a filling meal and a glass of good wine."

Flying Bat

Description
A large and lavishly appointed stone building with several levels stands before you. Inside, many different rooms can be found; from a rough-and-tumble taproom, to magnificent and lively dance halls, and everything in between. The common thread through it all is the exotic furnishings, collected from a lifetime of adventures across many cultures.

A Bit O' History
The Flying Bat was once a private club only for the rich, powerful and corrupt. After a group of adventurers had accumulated enough wealth from questing to purchase the deed from under them, they opened it to the public, and it has become a huge success. It's an establishment that encourages and celebrates diversity, even the waiters dress as misunderstood creatures such as vampires and goblins, though their costumes look a little too realistic.

Reviews
Lord Mayorton 5/5
"What an amazing place the food, drink, the songs! Where do they find such inhumanly stunning ladies?"

Lady Mayorton 3/5
"Dreadfully poor taste, I say! They let just anyone come in here. And those 'ladies' that get my husband all flustered."

Fud

Description

Described as the most decadent tavern in all the land, a blend of marble and fine oak, embellished with gold leaf designs and other finery. Many of the common-folk deem this place too expensive and rarely visit, except for special occasions. The tavern's name, pronounced 'F-YU-D' is often mispronounced by the commoners as 'FUD.' Through the main doors, a breathtaking foyer splits off into several directions leading to the restaurant and bar - a place filled with fine merchants – as well as a plush inn and spa.

A Bit O' History

Fud was founded by the world-renowned chef, Wolfe, a being from the fire plane who worked his way up from his humble beginnings as a street food vendor. He wanted to create the greatest premium guest experience imaginable. He now owns one of the grandest buildings in the whole city. Along with his staff - his trusted maître d', Monsieur Moustache; the house Mixologist, Brad, and many fire-hardened chefs - Wolfe is king of the high-end tavern world.

Reviews

Lord Farthingham 5/5
"Simply the greatest and most decadent experience I've ever had."

Grom the Barbarian 1/5
"Would not let me in because 'I didn't meet the dress code.' Bunch of namby-pamby prissy faces!"

Gaststuben of Aventurien

Description
Nestled alongside many other Dwarven taverns, with each one boasting its specialties in cooking and brewing, the tavern was built from an old Dwarven fishing vessel; hence why its decor celebrates generations of Dwarven fisherman. Nets and sail canvases extend from the building, forming canopies above the busy outdoor seating area where the staff attentively provides patrons with food and drink. The floors are scrubbed clean, and you feel as though you are standing in the captain's quarters of a wealthy sailor.

A Bit O' History
Built by a dwarf named Kubax, son of Doro, who sailed the world like his fisherman father, but did so for adventure instead. When he decided it was time to hang up his axe he brought his taste for adventure home while honouring his father's legacy; the taverns speciality is cooked fish served with your choice of ale or spiced tea. The taverns in the surrounding district compete against each other annually to put their cooking and brewing to the test.

Reviews
Sigismer Nesselmoor 4/5
"This is the perfect place for any traveller if you want to taste a dish from home or if you want to know how the food and beer will taste at the place you travel next."

The Gilded Rose

Description

The Rose is a modestly-sized tavern that from the outside could be mistaken for an inn. Inside, lights are always flickering and you can hear laughter at all hours of the day. Warm and inviting, the inside is modestly decorated and as well maintained as a hall full of rowdy patrons can be. All tables and chairs face towards the main stage as nightly entertainment is on offer, with the bouncers in the back always watching the customers for trouble.

A Bit O' History

Though a front for the local Thieves' Guild The Rose has become something of a resident destination for a specific kind of entertainment. Scantily clad waitresses and exotic performers have made this tavern a name, for better or for worse, but the customers – and more importantly the staff – are happy. Owned and run by a gnome who gave up a life on the road, this thief now trades in secrets and treasures, as well as the occasional bounty when the guild calls for it. Be careful though, he is very protective of his girls and won't hesitate to have his bouncers toss you out for getting too handsy, or corner you in some dark alley for skimping on that bill.

Reviews

Qacik Ravenwillow 2/5

"Not wing or talon friendly. And the owner only pays attention to the highest paying customers; so don't look for help unless you have the gold. It needs more variety in drinks, too much local brew."

The Griffin's Quill

 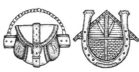

Description

From the outside, it appears to be your average tavern, but on the inside, the large dining benches are surrounded by enormous bookshelves, crammed with tomes from across the land. Along one wall, you see three cartography tables, strewn with equipment and maps. This tavern is a haven for scholars of all shapes and sizes.

A Bit O' History

The Griffin's Quill has existed for longer than anyone can recall and its location is documented in the oldest historical texts. At any time you can find all manner of folk wanting to decipher a cryptic message or research the whereabouts of an old dungeon. Many come to discuss ideas, lore and recently discovered lands. This is a tavern for those seeking answers to the rarest of questions, or to add to the shelves of knowledge. Usually, there will be someone who knows the location of the book or parchment you are trying to find.

Reviews

Dar of Boggymeadow 1/5
"I found an old boot. I went to get it appraised in case it was of value, and the entire place ridiculed me. I'll never go back!"

Kaleth the Cleaver 5/5
"Old Ransair found me exactly the right incantation I needed to open the sealed urn I acquired from a bothersome Orc chieftain."

Hole in the Wall

Description
Between the crowded houses near the city wall lies a small, strange-looking door, and behind this door is a quaint little tavern. The patrons appear to be mostly older wizards and witches. The interior features wooden beams and oak flooring, reminiscent of an old crawl space. Small benches covered in mismatching cushions and rugs sit in little nooks around the bar, and the shelves are lined with dusty books.

A Bit O' History
Once a haven for oppressed magic users at times of war, this small hideaway later became a legitimate watering hole. It remains fairly hidden due to the nature of its clientele, but is now a favourite spot for locals and an excellent place to learn a spell, devotion, or a curse or two.

Reviews
Myson the Magnificent 5/5
"A great place to meet some of the magic communities more, 'eccentric' characters. A bit of music would be nice though."

Jack Je-Peu 4/5
"If there were rooms I'd quite literally live here. Some of my greatest experiments have come from drinking here first."

Minotaur's Horns

Description
The auburn brick and cherry wooden three-story building appears old but well maintained in this affluent part of the city. Laughter and music can be heard emanating from the walls. Inside the main taproom, you find an expansive bar, a kitchen, a hearth and plenty of seating. Beyond this room, you may see a smaller bar area known as the "Arse o' the Beast," a space reserved for nobles and wealthy customers.

A Bit O' History
Founded by a group of adventurers that survived a devastating encounter, the story changes every time. The tavern is renowned for its friendly atmosphere and comfortable locale. It is a place where all are welcome, and for finding what you seek. The staff includes: Dhara, the red-haired Half elven waitress; Belryl "Grumps" Rockcleave, the balding, grey-haired, Dwarven bartender; and Mik, the human, raven-haired "ambassador" of entertainment.

Reviews
Elyrl Evercloak 5/5
"I always stop off at 'The Horns'. Great times, great food! And they had all the spell components I needed. You won't be unsatisfied."

Dorm Giantslayer 4/5
"As a dwarf, I can rarely find a place that caters to my needs. But I highly recommend the Horns! Oh, I never give a 5..."

Staff and Patrons of Minotaur's Horns

Khairn "The Mighty" (Minotaur: Owner)
Khairn stands well over seven feet tall. He has large black eyes and soft, crimson hair that coats his body. His horns are sharp and are as black as polished onyx. His expression is one of perpetual amusement.

Likes: Cooking, conversation Dislikes: Arrogance, impoliteness Wants: Everyone to enjoy themselves	Fears: True evil and unable to help those in need Flaws: Too trusting

Belryl "Grumps" Rockcleave (Dwarf: Bartender)
Belryl is an old, wrinkled, balding, grey-haired, mountain dwarf who looks like the years have been not kind to him. What once was muscle has turned to fat. He's not as quick as he used to be but he can still be formidable if needed.

Likes: A drink, a song Dislikes: People Wants: News and gossip	Fears: Dying alone, being unable to protect his friends Flaws: Gruff, grumpy, slow

Dhara Scarletmantle (Half elf: Bar Staff)
Dhara is a beautiful Half elven waitress, with an easy smile and a friendly face. She has long, flowing, red hair that falls around her shoulders. Her green eyes glint with mischief, and she has a soft laugh that sounds almost musical.

Likes: Helping people with drinks, food Dislikes: Being touched Wants: Information/ knowledge	Fears: Outliving her friends Flaws: Easily distracted

Ogre's Armpit

Description

A ramshackle residence looms ominously before you. You may have heard rumours of this establishment. If so, you will most likely stride past the entrance. Even from the street, the stench of The Ogre's Armpit assails your nostrils. Once named the best tavern in all of Serendipity, inhabitants of the city soon worked out the review was from The Guild of Murder Hobos.

A Bit O' History

The oldest tavern in the city, The Ogress was a den of inequities burnt down in the great fire of the Gnomish Inquisition. Nobody expected it. Even less expected was the rebuild, funded by The Guild of Murder Hobos. Beneath the new tavern is The Basement of Doom, where patrons play games of chance with chainsaws, and a healthy disregard for safety.

Reviews

Vok Wightkicker 3/5

"The beer is cold, and the crisps are salty. What more do I need? Oh, it's peaceful enough. Trouble has a hard time getting started with a rock Troll on the door."

The Pilfered Drum

Description

The large brick and wood-beamed building before you has clearly endured its fair share of catastrophe. Though the entrance looks brand new, the rest of the building looks in dire need of repair and scorch marks can be seen around the windows. On the inside, the straw on the floor barely covers the blood and beer stains from the previous night, and mean looking ruffians occupy the cheap looking furniture. A single bartender behind a long ramshackle bar eyes you with contempt as you approach.

A Bit O' History

Stolen from another owner, the Pilfered Drum has yet to improve its reputation. Bards and music of most types are discouraged, as the patrons tend to consider the artists as moving targets. The meanest of the mean tend to frequent the establishment, and if you upset one you are considered suicidal, as its patrons will kindly oblige your need for death's embrace.

Reviews

Rins Wand 3/5

"The ale is nearly as good as the fried potato, and the staff put out nuts sometimes."

Drikthe 1/5

"The other patrons are brutishly rude, dirty and ugly. The beer was so nasty that it burned a hole in the table."

The Promise

Description
Wedged between single-story, unpainted, wooden shacks along a dirt street, the smell of human refuse overpowers the senses as you approach. The only way to distinguish The Promise from the other ramshackle shops and dwellings is a towering symbol of a wave curling over a star, which hangs above an ill-fitting door. You see the hints of cheap food and drink - and the hints of a brawl or two inside the old tavern.

A Bit O' History
A seedy bar where the disenfranchised people of the city congregate to drink cheap swill at night, and sleep it off on the floor during the day. The residents of the area are not friendly towards non-humans and rumour has it that this tavern serves as a recruiting station for a violent cult known as 'The Black Cloaks.' No one knows the purpose of this cult, but it seems they prey on the needy and destitute, enlisting them to do their bidding with the promise of a better life.

Reviews
Conan the Librarian 1/5
"The unlearned, ill-mannered, and frankly aesthetically-lacking denizens of The Promise tarnish this city for all non-humans."

Grencha Wriathwhite 1/5
"I only go to The Promise 'cuz it's close. If you're not human, don't go. Other than that, the drink is cheap."

Staff and Patrons of The Promise

The Recruiter (Human: Cultist)
The Recruiter is a shadowy human who wears expensive black robes and frequents The Promise to look for desperate human patrons. His recruits receive cheap black cloaks to wear and assignments to perform. The patrons and locals fear him, and more so by his recruits.

Likes: Young, unhappy men Dislikes: Women, non-humans Wants: Minions and power	Fears: Agents of other cults Flaws: Arrogant and selfish

Grencha Wriathwhite (Human: Costume Shop Owner)
Grencha is a stout, unassuming old woman who looks like her best days are behind her. She frequently, and expertly, wears a wig of bright red hair, which covers her own rather wispy head of silver.

Likes: Halfling sweet tobacco Dislikes: Gnomes, half-orcs, half-elves, most full elves Wants: Better source for wigs	Fears: Being uncovered as a sorcerer Flaws: Quite racist, often overly perfectionist

Father Cornelius Vee (Human: Priest)
Father Cornelius Vee is an elderly Human priest who wears wine-coloured robes and serves in the local temple. He's part greeter, part counsellor, and part apothecary, with his remedies for hangovers and other party-related maladies proving popular. He makes the rounds of the various taverns, inns, and restaurants to offer the services of his temple.

Likes: Drinking and partying Dislikes: Prohibitionists Wants: Parties, to find his cat	Fears: The King or City Guard Flaws: Memory

The Rusted Anchor

Description
The large sailing vessel draws the attention of many as it sails slowly past the port, with the call of its captain announcing the day's special events and offers. Many people can be seen jumping on, and stumbling off, the gangway. Below the main deck, its portholes glow and shine with the promise of good food and entertainment.

A Bit O' History
The tavern was originally called 'The Portside Tavern' until its anchor rusted and sent the ship on its eternal voyage. The owner found it more lucrative to sail around the surrounding towns picking up and dropping off patrons, so he never moored the ship again. The vessel sticks to a strict schedule and never stops sailing. Patrons must enter and leave the tavern as it crawls past ports.

Reviews
Tidus Moongrave 3/5
"I joined the boat for a quiet drink and lost four days! Great food! Great wine! Great Bards!"

Finn Bluehand 2/5
"I sometimes wish it stayed in one place; I missed the boat again!"

The Rusty Mug

Description
This rough and tumble tavern is perfect for the average adventurer that is just looking for some ale and basic food, such as bread and dried meats. At the back of the tavern, you can find a ring that is used for nightly entertainment, and endless bouts of brawn and bravery. The Rusty Mug is a great place to seek an adventurer for hire, or to hear about local gossip and news from afar. The regulars that frequent the tavern who complete quests for the locals have their names on the walls with a scoreboard beneath them.

A Bit O' History
This tavern was created by two brothers who are former Knights of the Realm. Darran and Thomas Mug opened this tavern as a cheap place for adventurers to rest their heads, and a way for would-be heroes to find an excellent adventure to keep them occupied.

Reviews
Aron MusterGlove 2/5
"Not a great place to stay but the ale was fresh, and the entertainment was... interesting. I found a few jobs that will work for now until I find an adventure that best suits me and Colonel Muster."

Winston R. Taycall 5/5
"Best place I've been to in a while. The bed was soft, and the pockets were easy to pick, I walked out with more than I came with... I'll make sure to stop back on my way through again."

The Sanguine Fox

Description
The Fox is a private sodality for shapeshifters run by Mitsuki Gizensha. After placing your hand or paw upon the wryly grinning fox on the door, you find it opens. Inside, you are asked to relinquish all weaponry and are reminded not to cause any disturbances. The opulent common room boasts many tables with comfortable chairs, couches, and floor pillows. Upstairs you will find private rooms, as well as bathing areas. The Fox is a place of peace and provides the opportunity to rest, with many amenities available to its clientele.

A Bit O' History
All therianthropes are welcome no matter their breed, and Mitsuki determines the rules – as well as deciding who has broken them. Nika Dragomirov, a polymorphed female dragon, will 'escort' troublemakers to the local law enforcement if you're lucky. The Fox was established as a place of refuge solely for therianthropes. Only those who have violated the rules are ever turned away. Regular beings are generally not allowed unless dictated by either Mitsuki or Nika.

Reviews
Benveuto Rourke 4/5
"Excellent food and rooms, though it can be frustrating when your bounty is also making use of the services."

The Scales of Fate

Description
The interior of this fine looking establishment is always dim, with heavy curtains covering the windows. Candles flicker at every table and booth, with well-dressed waiters bouncing from table to table. Bars sit at both ends of the establishment with several secluded booths framing the outside edge of the main floor. One bar showcases vintage wines and spirits, the other a selection of exotic teas.

A Bit O' History
The Scales is an upscale establishment, known for its high-quality beverage selection. The owner is a skinny lizard-man adorned with fine clothing and a monocle named Sauriv ihk Irthosi. The Scales host many private functions and the customer's privacy is of utmost concern to Sauriv. He knows the rumours concerning shady deals being conducted here, but no one dares say a thing. The staff are privy to the darkest secrets shared at these tables; some of the team may part with some of the more nefarious rumours for a price.

Reviews
Carver Koenig 5/5
"Great place to find new and exciting teas! The wine selection is also excellent if you're trying to show someone a grand time."

Grogmar Stonebleeder 2/5
"Whiskey was tolerable but far too much for my taste. Let a dwarf drink in peace without being pestered over silly Elvish wines!"

Treble Clef Tavern

Description
The sound of music drifts from the open door of the Treble Clef Tavern, a clean looking wood-beamed building stands before you. A beautiful voice is captivating and alluring as you cross the threshold. Everyone inside is transfixed by the performer on the stage, including both the bartenders and the patrons. The furniture is arranged to focus all attention on the stage, and no one is talking, only listening.

A Bit O' History
The tavern was established by a group of bards looking to provide a stage for the many talents that visit the city. Night and day, stories, songs, and poems are performed in front of an attentive audience that appreciates the art of songs and sonnets. A selection of fine beverages is provided during performances, but talking is not permitted until each act has finished.

Reviews
Primus Secundus III 5/5
"Excellent performances this evening, really expressive. One piece in particular portrayed a superb commentary of the idealistic paradigm of the socio-political structure."

Bill Brighthorn 1/5
"What did I walk in to? No one was talking except the person on stage wearing no clothes and talking with his belly button?"

The Yellow King

Description
The sign above the door depicts a figure with its head bowed, shadowed in a cowl, and dressed in tattered yellow robes, with a small diadem on its head. The shadows behind the figure almost seem to suggest wings. The public bar is always thronged but feels deserted as the patrons stare with sullen faces into their greasy tankards and glasses, sitting alone or in small groups of two or three. An air of desperation tinged with menace pervades the room.

A Bit O' History
Although primarily where people go to drink and forget, this is the sort of establishment where one can make arrangements for journeys to distant parts of the realm. In the dark corners of the tavern, you can find the evil creatures of the city. With a proper introduction, one can buy influence through blackmail and coercion, but the price is often more than mere coin.

Reviews
Hildred Castaigne 2/5
"You will never find a more wretched hive of scum and villainy than the Yellow King, but for those seeking special services, it can prove surprisingly rewarding if you know the right people to ask. Although most of the residents are content to wallow in their despair."

The Yellow Pinwheel

Description
The tavern is a large establishment taking up half a city block. Outside, above the door, is a giant yellow pinwheel that is designed to turn when the wind is strong enough. Inside, the lighting is kept dim with tables throughout most of the room. Along the back wall there is a long bar where drinks are served, next to which a door leads to the kitchen and a changing room for the entertainers. There is a stairway leading down to the basement where many bedrooms are available to rent.

A Bit O' History
Ever since the enemy has occupied the country, the Yellow Pinwheel is the central base of operations for the resistance. The prostitutes that work there have been recruited into the resistance and use their "interpersonal skills" to acquire information whenever possible. One of the bedrooms in the basement contains a secret door to the underground base of operations for the resistance. The Yellow Pinwheel has an unblemished reputation and is often visited by both locals and members of the occupying army alike.

Reviews
Clementine Sanders 5/5
"Excellent atmosphere and the entertainment is top notch. They even stock Khaflorian Ale!! Highly recommended, I will return as soon as I'm able."

41

On the Road Taverns

From trade routes to barely-travelled paths, there is nearly always a place for a weary traveller to rest their boots and fill their stomach. While some establishments reap the benefits of travelling merchants and the flow of coin between cities, others barely make their living but still look after their patrons with devotion and attentive service.

Agarth's Ale Cart

Description
A sizeable horse-drawn cart loaded with barrels and small casks has stopped at the side of the road. A giant horse grazes as a well-dressed man hurriedly sets up his impromptu tavern. The rear of the cart has been opened to reveal a bar area complete with stools and drinkware. The simple wooden sign above the cart reads 'Agarth's Ale Cart'.

A Bit O' History
The Ale Cart was created by a rather eccentric, human, gentleman called Agarth Aleton, and the location is ever-changing. His knowledge and passion for ale and other forms of fermented hops is unrivalled. Agarth travels the realm in search of new and exciting beverages to take back to his flagship tavern, called Agarth's Brewhouse.

Reviews
Jonnas Hjolnik 4/5
"Had some brew from my hometown! Never thought I'd taste that sweet nectar again!"

Torrin Norixius 2/5
"No food and no bards. I like beer and all, but I like my taverns to have something more!"

Ale Keep

Description

The Ale Keep, as its name implies, is housed in an old, stone castle. The outer walls are semi-intact, but the gatehouse is in ruins. A permanent bridge now crosses the old moat, which is fed by a large creek. The main floor of the keep houses the brewery, kitchens and taproom. The second floor contains rooms for rent, the top floor is used as private quarters, and the cellar is used for brewing and storage. Large private parties have been known to use the wall-walk atop the keep. Large hearths flank both ends of the enormous taproom and its long, polished purple-wood bar.

A Bit O' History

The Ale Keep began life as a fully-functional castle, guarding a long forgotten border. As the tides of time-shifted, and the usefulness of the keep faded, it fell into disrepair. The keep is said to be haunted, but the proprietors won't say if it's true or not.

Reviews

Baern Strongfist 5/5
"Mistress Jocosa knows her brews. You'll find only the finest ales and distilled spirits at the Ale Keep, the house specials, brewed on site, are the best."

Vrank Deadbasher 5/5
"Watch out for the big guy; he's biased against greenskins!"

Staff and Patrons of The Ale Keep

Jacosa (Half elf: Bar Staff)

Jacosa is of average height, with dark hair and pale skin. She has a scar from her left ear to her jawbone. She's usually found in soft leather breeches, a grey blouse, blue vest, and boots - when working she also wears a frilly apron, which is at odds with her other attire. She carries a mash-paddle with her everywhere. Jacosa is married to Kynwric.

Likes: Beer, bourbon, and food Dislikes: Ruffians, cheats, brawlers Wants: Safety, stability	Fears: Loss (life, family, home), spiders Flaws: Temperamental, stubborn

Kynwric (Human: Bar Staff)

Kynwric is a burly man of slightly above-average height; he has reddish-blonde hair and a full beard. He is broad of chest, and stoutly built, but his body is suffering from middle age. He usually wears a simple cloth tunic and trousers, leather braces, and leather boots.

Likes: Beer, food, pretty girls Dislikes: Orcs, goblins, etc. Wants: Peace and quiet, books	Fears: Growing old and weak Flaws: Quick to anger, stubborn

Krük Deepsinger (Half giant: Bar Staff)

Krük is one of the oddest sights to be seen in the tavern. A vast, hulking humanoid in brightly coloured clothes, with an equally flamboyant cloak slung about his shoulders, he holds a lute in his hands and has an axe sheathed on his back.

Likes: Music, beer, food, women Dislikes: Pretentious people Wants: Fame, beer	Fears: Being ignored or irrelevant Flaws: Very flamboyant

Anvil's Rest

Description
A cobblestone building sits beside the road with a column of smoke rising from the chimney and the forge placed at its side. The noise of hammer on steel welcomes your arrival as the smithy stops momentarily to greet you as you head for the door. The interior of the tavern is warm and clean, and a cheery human female approaches you. The tables are full of capable-looking, like-minded adventurers enjoying the food and drink this cosy tavern has to offer.

A Bit O' History
A human couple run the tavern with a handful of other staff. With comfortable rooms to rent, and good food and ale, this tavern is a popular choice for many adventurers. Anastasia runs the front of house and her husband, Remus, runs the forge. Many patrons choose to have their armour repaired and altered during their stay.

Reviews
U'thlak the large 2/5
"Beds much small! Cups tiny!"

Henry Poltice 4/5
"Couldn't ask for any more, good food and drink, beds were comfortable, and I had my sword sharpened while I slept!"

Bloody Dragon

Description
As you wander through the winding pathways of the festival powerful spices clash with the subtle fragrances of cakes and other sweets, as merchants shout their bargains and colourful cloth flaps in the breeze. The drink wagon is a welcome sight, with barrels adorning the back of the cart and The Bloody Dragon scrawled on the side in red in draconic writing.

A Bit O' History
The festival is a retirement plan started by a group of adventurers, along with some friends and a lot of merchants. Rumour has it The Bloody Dragon's name stems from one of the adventures the proprietors had; he stumbled into town, covered head to toe in blood and carrying a nearly dead companion over each shoulder, vowing never to adventure again. The barkeep of the Bloody Dragon says it is true, but you can always pay the storyteller to hear it for yourself.

Reviews
Rhys the Blacksmith 4/5
"Great time, the wife spent all her time looking at the cloths and the spices, the blacksmiths know their stuff, some Dwarven magic as well, I think."

Deryn the Blacksmith's Wife 1/5
"Terrible place, it gave my husband crazy ideas, he wanted to give them my jewelled necklace for some rusty old hammer."

Staff and Patrons of the Bloody Dragon

Kiroc (Red Half dragon: Storyteller)

This tall man wears simple armour and a sword at his waist. He sits at a table in front of the Bloody Dragon cart, telling a growing crowd about how Kasula, spent a week stopping a group of time wizards stealing all the jewellery in a town.

Likes: Travelling, telling stories Dislikes: Fire, thieves, trouble-makers Wants: Good stories, no trouble	Fears: Dragons, losing his friends, getting older Flaws: Contentment/lack of ambition, stubbornness, revenge

Kasula (Elf: Bartender)

The elf leaning against the cart is lithe, even compared to other elves. A smile rushes to his face as he greets patrons, pulls their pints and taking their money; usually all at the same time. He stops to talk to adventurers, asking about their quests and offering advice.

Likes: Wine, women, magic Dislikes: Being stuck in one place, boredom Wants: Adventure, action	Fears: Old age, inability, loneliness Flaws: Hurried, rarely thinks, overly trusting

Erramun (Human: Sorceress/Magic Shop Owner)

The tent near The Bloody Dragon is full of magical paraphernalia: staffs, wands, various colours of gemstone and anything else you can think of. The old woman herself sits at the back, just placing down a half-empty mug of ale.

Likes: Selling, magic Dislikes: Fools, quacks Wants: A quiet life, fewer aches, rare magical objects	Fears: Death Flaws: Memory, lack of patience

Burping Frog

Description

Built from logs, The Burping Frog stands out on the rocky cliff overlooking the sea. The popular bar is on the ground floor, filled with shiny tables and dirty glasses. The three upper levels contain a number of rooms accommodating a range of clients, from seafaring merchants, to husbands fleeing their wives. Around the back of the inn, a number of small rooms jut out irregularly from the rear wall.

A Bit O' History

Delightfully designed by the renowned architect Otto Lottofotto, the façade of this beautiful log inn conceals its somewhat shadier insides. The barkeep and owner, Murph Grubbles, takes pride in his work and constantly does his best to improve the tavern. He can often be seen cleaning the windows and polishing the benches. Inside, you can always find the washed-up, Dwarven comedian, Orsik Alehord, who is always "here until Thursday" and always recommends guests "try the rat pie. It's delicious". Local tradesmen, including the blacksmith Dyrk Lardsy and the carpenter Ghuras Lardsy, frequent the bar. Contrary to popular local suspicion, they aren't related.

Reviews

Dwigget Flergle 2/5

"The ale tastes like donkey urine. Not that I know what it tastes like."

Drunken Do Do

Description
The Drunken Dodo is a tavern fitting of its name; a two-story 'L' shaped building, its finely crafted wood buttresses and Dwarven crafted stone mason work intertwine to create this hub of love, sweat, and tears. There are two windows flanking the front door with distinctly Elven carvings woven into the door design.

A Bit O' History
The Drunken Dodo was founded by a young (by elf standards) Elven boy, Berry Tinkle. Decades before, he had lived the life of an adventurer only to have witnessed something truly tragic, with most of his adventuring band having been wiped out. This left poor Berry hollow inside, and he sought something much more mundane to live out his years.

Reviews
Bianca 1/5
"It was loud and distasteful, but come to think of it that could have just been me. I do get like that after a few drinks."

Slamlord Sodasopa 4/5
"I found the tavern to be much to my liking. There was a large hearth which Berry allowed me to use to keep this giant blue rock I found warm."

Emerald Lily

Description

The Emerald Lilly can be seen from the road sitting on a small island in the middle of a still lake, the music dances across from the tavern to your ears. It stands as a small shack surrounded by tables and chairs, a jetty sits on one side of the island for travellers to row out too. The tavern serves strictly vegetarian cuisine harvested from the surrounding area but is best known for its Lilly liquor, an astoundingly potent liquid. Despite its modest appearance several members of staff can be seen milling about tending to its patrons.

A Bit O' History

Owned by an enchanting man named Salrah, he has much knowledge of the local area and is rumoured to have explored a local dungeon but is loath to speak of it. It has become common knowledge that the owner will happily accept bottles of liquor in exchange for services in order to keep the bar stocked. The tavern is under the protection and constant observation of an orge that carries a strange 'sentient' club that looks suspiciously like a stalactite, but the orge maintains that it is just a magic club.

Reviews

Princess Eloria Shallowspear 1/5
"Yuck. Don't mess with the bouncer or you will find yourself tossed into the lake. Only room for a dozen or so."

Forgotten Stronghold

Description

The Forgotten Stronghold is the last sign of civilization along the road. It is built within the ruins of an old fortress. While the main keep is still standing, the wall and towers surrounding it have crumbled. One tower along the wall still remains, and you can see the glow of a forge and hear the rhythmic sound of a hammer upon steel.

Outside of the keep, you see wagons of travellers, as well as tents and temporary merchant stands. As you enter the keep and ascend the stairs you are greeted by a half-orc that gives you a quick visual inspection before letting you enter the great hall. At the far end of the hall there is a large fireplace, and most evenings there will be performers near it playing.

A Bit O' History

The tavern occupies an old outpost on the edge of the wilds. The current owner is a halfling named Madrigal, who goes by Mads, and can always be found behind the bar serving drinks and trading tales of adventure with the patrons. One will notice that the servers and cooks are mostly made up of half-orcs, and that any patron deciding to cause trouble will promptly be shown the door.

Reviews

Fimnil Oakenborn 4/5

"The rooms were a bit drafty, but the food and ale was the good and there was plenty of it."

Giant's Last Rest

Description

You see before you a fine, timber building with brightly-coloured plasterwork adorning its exterior. The exposed timber frame has been delicately carved throughout the two main wings that hug the courtyard. The grounds of the inn house include; a vast herb garden, a well, a modest stable and a flagstone patio. The welcoming building doesn't disappoint as you head into the main bar area, with the smell of stew filling your nose as you eye the selection of beverages on offer behind the bar. The other thing that catches your eye as you enter is a giant, chain hauberk that hangs above the hearth.

A Bit O' History

This tavern was bought by three adventurers: Cecily, Phelman, and Reydzog. They raised the funds by selling the armour of a storm giant they had slain, but the hauberk remains above the fireplace. As local heroes, they also offer rooms to rent that are named and designed after each of them. The Cecily room is decidedly feminine, with a quiet aesthetic.

Reviews

Targi Shanin, Latro 3/5
"The owners are latro, you'd think they would offer a price break. Service is quick, and the road stew is filling."

Hasselwhite's Vulgar Vicar

Description
Around a bend in the road a few days' travel from anywhere
noteworthy lies a well-made tavern of rough-hewn ironwood
and warm fires. Placed invitingly in a large meadow,
surrounded by numerous outbuildings, Hasselwhite's Vulgar
Vicar doesn't so much welcome you as it wraps your weary
soul in a soothing liniment smelling of mint and eucalyptus.
But everything has a price here, and they do mean everything.

A Bit O' History
Hasselwhite has been a tavern proprietor for many years.
Owned by a stunningly foul-mouthed halfling of indefinite
lineage and impeccable connections. The Vulgar Vicar is his
latest venture, founded soon after he was run out of The
Horn following a quarrel with the Thieves' Guild, and
presumably far enough away for a fresh start. The steady
muscle behind the bar is a man known as Smithsohn O'Malley.

Reviews
Lady Diana Orlen 4 /5
*"The Vicar is my go-to, you can always meet a new connection here.
But if that idiot Hasselwhite pinches my bottom one more time, not
even Smithsohn will be able to salvage the situation."*

Madrigal Jack 3/5
*"Double-knot your belt purse because you can get anything you need
here — as long as you can pay for it."*

Staff and Patrons of Hasselwhite's Vulgar Vicar

Tolman Hasselwhite (Halfling: Tavern Proprietor)

Stout for a halfling, with constantly dishevelled hair, Tolman Hasselwhite has the foulest mouth this side of the Nine Hells, making sailors sound like priestesses of the Mother Goddess. And he is always hustling an angle. He knows everyone, has connections everywhere and can get just about anything given enough time and money. He's also irritated every major player in his network at one time or another. But people keep coming back to him because he gets results.

Likes: Cursing, making a deal, tall redheads, and political history books Dislikes: Spiders, liars Wants: Gold, power, fame	Fears: Missing a deal Flaws: Cursing, and has a soft spot for tall redheads

Smithsohn O'Malley (Human: Barkeep)

Tall, broad, taciturn, exuding quiet competence and unexpected grace; Smithsohn O'Malley is a quiet antidote to Hasselwhite's irreverent bluster. O'Malley never talks about his background or how he got entangled with Hasselwhite, but the scars tell a tale of a man familiar with the application of violence to influence outcomes. Anyone familiar with political history might recognise the tattoo on his arm as one only given to elite warriors from a distant northern land.

Likes: Symphonies, good deeds, stories, gourmet meals Dislikes: Dishonesty, bluster and braggarts Wants: Peace and quiet	Fears: Nothing Flaws: Perhaps he's too loyal to Hasselwhite

Hunter's Rest

Description
The tavern before you resembles a wooden hunting lodge, a metal sign above the door depicts a humanoid figure wielding a bow and arrow. The main bar area is large but cosy, fur rugs and pelts from the hunt adorn the floors and walls. A bard lazily strums his lute by the fire that gives the room a distinctly smoky atmosphere. The barkeep looks to be more interested in counting his coin than clearing the empty mugs and plates that lay about the place.

A Bit O' History
What was once a hunter's retreat used to house trophies and equipment now stands as a shadow of its former self. Some of the best hunters in the land would gather here and trade and swap tales of ferocious beasts before it was sold suddenly to a greedy barkeep. Rumour has it that the building is haunted by a ranger that was injured in a hunting accident, hence its quick sale - but most would argue that this is poppycock.

Reviews
Ellie Silver-heart 3/5
"A small inn but a nice place to have a drink on the road, could be improved."

Eloea 2/5
"The ale is watered down and the food is awful."

Logan's Bog

Description
A short distance from the neighbouring city, the overgrown and mossy roof of a stone tavern called Logan's Bog can be found. Fogged windows flicker with the glow of a warm fire, calling from inside, and the rumble of conversation and glasses clanking can be heard from the main roads. Inside, everything is made from beer stained wood. Logan, the owner, only serves beer that she brews and has developed quite a reputation for being the best brewer in the area.

A Bit O' History
After years of adventure, Logan found that every day behind her bar was an adventure. She took shelter there when it was just an abandoned house and never left. Over time the house became a home, then, after news of her home-brewed beer reached the city, her home became a tavern. On a wooden board behind the bar, a sign reads: "One Rule! Take it outside!" Not once has there been a fight within the Bog, but the doorstep has seen its fair share.

Reviews
Aneres 4/5
"My second home, best beer I've ever had. I will likely die in this very seat."

88 3/5
"I run a business and meet my customers here. They love it."

Lucky Raven

Description
The tavern before you seems to have been recently built, with a smithy also being built next to it. Above the door of the slate-roofed tavern sits a sign depicting a raven grasping a cloverleaf. The upper floor boasts a large balcony wreathed in plants and wildflowers. The inside is as lush and new as you would expect from the outside, packed with patrons looking for refreshments and rest. The staff appear well dressed and are hurriedly meeting the demands of the customers.

A Bit O' History
Started by Gregor, and his wife Eleanor (the barkeep and cook), a few years ago the Lucky Raven is the latest of many taverns run by his extensive family. Located near a new trade route, business is booming. Thanks to its wide network, the family prides itself on always having new and exotic dishes on the menu. They run a tight ship and their staff are always friendly and attentive.

Reviews
Leif Sigmarsson 5/5
"The food is fair enough, but this is one of the few places along this road where I had a good night sleep without being worried about robbers."

Sean McDraenor 2/5
"Good food, fresh beds, and good entertainment. Don't touch the barmaids though!"

Staff and Patrons of The Lucky Raven

Gregor Splatinovicz (Human: Tavern Owner)

Clean-shaven, charismatic, and with striking blue eyes, Gregor is the clear centre of the tavern. Obviously deeply in love with his wife Eleanor, he strives to make the tavern a happy place. Despite his occupation, he is not as impressed by rich and powerful visitors as a regular tavern owner should be.

Likes: Exotic food and drink Dislikes: Rudeness Wants: Children, the Sixth Amulet of Xiang Feng	Fears: Disappointing his uncle Flaws: Obsessive about keeping the tavern clean

Liao Wan Cheng (Human: Stable Master)

Jovial and grey-haired, he welcomes everyone in his stables and will take very good care of their animals. Anyone disturbing the animals or trying to steal from the parked wagons will find he has talent with a quarterstaff.

Likes: Animals, gardening Dislikes: People hurting animals Wants: A striped mountain parrot	Fears: Necromancy Flaws: Obsessive collector of religious texts

Lily Traendhal (Half Elf: Barmaid)

Lily (like her twin sister Mimi) is a slender and beautiful girl. Even at the busiest hour, she'll nimbly weave through the crowd. Her quick hands and quick wit give you the impression she has done more than work in a tavern during her life.

Likes: Darts, fine silk and jewellery Dislikes: Being touched Wants: Black Opal of Xiliphon	Fears: Her great-great-grand-father Flaws: She does not lose at darts

Morden's Cider Alley

Description

The main room before you is a long hall with large casks mounted in the walls on the left and a dark wooden bar to the right. There is enough seating for hundreds of travellers, all on long tables with stools. An enormous hearth with a roaring fire is at the very end of the hall, and the smell of roasting meat and potatoes fills the air.

A Bit O' History

Morden's Cider Hall was opened by retired adventurer Francis "Tank" Morden when he hung up his glaive and settled down here in the mountains. Tank earned his fortune through his adventures, as well as a handful of smart investments in mines and armouries in towns he visited. He runs the Hall and can be found sitting by the fire telling stories of his battles with dragon cultists, while his wife, Haley, runs the business from behind the bar. Tank's sons are also involved in the business – Iago is the blacksmith and his younger sibling Viet will likely stable your horses. Both resemble their father in stature and brooding manner; so haggle at your own peril. It's rumoured that Zhentarim used this beer hall as a drop location, but asking about that will likely get you killed.

Reviews

Grigor Mansplain 5/5

"Best food and drink in the realm! And if you ask Tank nicely, he'll take you down to his trophy room and show you the artefacts he collected before he took that arrow in the knee."

Oink 'n' Boinkberry

Description

Slightly off the beaten path lies a conglomerate of mud daub huts and a ramshackle barn with red paint peeling off in the sunlight. From the outside, the huts all appear to be connected to each other by rickety wooden hallways that seem as if they would fall over, given a strong wind.
A musky aroma emanates from the barn area, and the sound of hoofs and a variety of animal noises can be heard, along with occasional swearing and shouting.

A Bit O' History

The Oink'n'Boink is infamous for barmaids of negotiable virtue, and a thriving illicit market kept mostly in the shadows and available to anyone that asks. Dishes such as Boinkinberry pie and Oinkers'n'Mash can be acquired at the inn as well as horrendous ale. Far from most civilisation, it tends to be left to its villainous activities.

Reviews

Marty the Sneak 4/5
"The most wretched hive of scum and villainy ever seen. It's a truly magical place. Stay away from the Boinkinberry pie, there ain't no Boinkinberries in it."

Mortin the Mighty Magnificent 1/5
"Flea-ridden hidey-hole between two small villages. It's the only real stop and at least it doesn't leak."

Prancing Mare

Description
A simple tavern made from wood and stone, the dancing mare has stood on the road for many years. It offers the basic comforts required of merchants and adventurers alike. It sits away from most of the usual trade roads but receives a steady amount of patronage, making most of its money tending to the horses of travellers and repairing merchant wagons.

A Bit O' History
Built while the surrounding towns were thriving with gold, trade and minerals, it now exists as a simple stop for refreshments and sanctuary. No longer used as often as it once was, it sits on a longer route to the main trading cities. Its main clientele are smaller merchants who wish to trade goods to the smaller villages in the area.

Reviews
Blodwin Pinto 3/5
"A bit outta the way but it's a welcome sight considering the main route is closed at the moment."

Pilla Telst 2/5
"Still not sure how I ended up here."

Tipsy Titan

Description
Nestled high on a well-travelled mountain pass, this converted ancient Dwarven fortress is enormous. Cut into the stone of the mountain itself, with high walls and a sturdy gate, guards welcome you into a large cobblestone courtyard, with a stable and warehouse for storing merchant wagons. The tavern has a large, stone common room with large fire pits and plenty of seating. A fat halfling and his kitchen hands run its busy kitchen, and the second floor offers a large library for the guests to relax in, which has a far more subdued tone to the common room downstairs.

A Bit O' History
Boronar Bloodbeard was given the Inn by his uncle. The name refers to an incident several thousand years ago, which involved a Titan making his own wine and getting very drunk. The wine still exists, legends say, and is very rare, valuable and tasty. The cellar beneath the tavern has three levels filled with food and drink. Rumour has it the third level has an entrance into the dark caverns of the mountain.

Reviews
Alagar 4/5
"The perfect place to rest after a long hard trek up the mountain pass. Good food, plenty of ale a jolly atmosphere with reasonably priced rooms."

Village Taverns

At first glance, the sleepy little villages that grace this realm may appear boring and sedate, but at the heart of every village lies a roaring tavern or two. Filled with the lifeblood of the village, these little treasures are bursting with local information and rumour.

So enjoy your ale, chat with the locals and take in your surroundings, because it won't be long before you find yourself knee deep in trouble.

Agarth's Brewhouse

Description
A beautifully simple building of wood and stone stands next to a large warehouse. Smoke rises from the chimneys filling the air with a mixture of fine cooking and brewing hops. The tavern itself is a museum of brewing history combined with a functional tavern, and a range of ales are readily available along with home-cooked meals.

A Bit O' History
Owned by an eccentric ale expert known as Agarth, the tavern serves as a focal point for any ale pilgrimage. The owner is rarely found here, however, as he is usually travelling the realm searching for new brewing techniques or fine ales to bring to his tavern. A small number of well-trained staff attend to the needs of patrons and can provide any information or materials needed to brew beer. Patrons are also invited to take a tour of the brew house situated next to the tavern.

Reviews
Jonnas Hjolnik 4/5
"After meeting Agarth on the road I just had to come here. It's beautiful"

Bard and Brew

Description
The Bard and Brew sits as the last building on the way out of town; the last distraction before heading off on a dangerous quest, and also the first sight to welcome you back. The walls and roof are simple and aged, but thick and strong. More than once it has served as the first defence of the town. The building itself is fairly large with the first-floor set higher than usual. The windows provide light but, due to their lofty placement, they make it difficult for those wishing to enter the establishment for less than savoury purposes.

A Bit O' History
Founded by a retired adventuring party after the loss of two of its members to a dangerous foe, the remaining three chose to use their gains and settle down, so to speak. Adventure still finds them often enough, but at least they can control their impulses now. Having a skilled bard to soothe rowdy customers and a skilled alchemist helps their reputation.

Reviews
Thoradin Redbeard 3/5
"The Bard and Brew isn't the biggest or the best, but the fire is warm and the ale flows. It could use an extra bouncer on weekends though."

Berrian Merrianme 3/5
"Comfortable enough, I guess. I would like to see a more varied spirit and menu selection."

Damaged Daffodil

Description
The banner of a daffodil crushed under a spiked mace hangs above the door. The inn stands two stories tall under a weathered, thatched roof. It looks in good repair yet covered in deep, green moss. A balcony juts out over the main doorway providing shelter to patrons as they enter during times of poor weather, with the balcony itself providing an excellent view of the village when the weather is fair. The building has no distinguishing features except the carving of a Dwarven face found on the large oak double door that stands proudly at the entrance.

A Bit O' History
A female dwarf runs the inn, a little shorter than your average dwarf, she walks on a raised platform behind the bar shouting orders to her staff. Her staff all appear to be attractive human men, all scurrying around looking to avoid chastisement from their employer. She seems to enjoy the power she has over them.

Reviews
Grum Bridgewater 4/5
"Excellent little place to grab a drink. That dwarf is a feisty one!"

Brent Crossmane 2/5
"Nice location, nice food, and drink. Couldn't relax on account of the shouting from that woman behind the bar."

Dock & Dory

Description
A small, two story building, neatly kept. The cry of seagulls and the smell of salt water fill the air. The door to the establishment is open, and the sounds of laughter and fiddling drift through the door. Behind the tavern, is a fair-sized L shaped dock, which is nearly 100 ft in length.

A Bit O' History
Known by the locals as the "Dark & Dirty" the tavern serves as the main watering hole for the local fishing village. The main customers are hardworking fishermen and their families. Occasionally there may be a few shadier characters mixed in amongst the patrons.

The proprietors are a middle-aged human couple, one a former fisherman until an injury caused him to retire. The drink and food is local fair, but occasionally they get their hands on more exotic liquor.

Reviews
Oliver 2/5
"The rooms left a lot to be desired. Straw mattresses! The local drink was serviceable, but an old one-eyed patron kept calling me "old son" all night!"

Gwynifer Highstrider 4/5
"Always love stopping in after a long sail! The ale is frothy, the beds are comfy, and the music is lively! If only we had more room to dance!"

Drunken Spoon

Description
The Drunken Spoon is far more than the name suggests. The tavern lies amidst a quiet looking village near a well-travelled trade route. The astonishingly clean tavern made of stone, clay, and wood caters to swarms of travellers every day. Inside, trophies from various adventures are hung on every available space, and the smell of well-cooked food stifles the aroma of merchants that have been on the road for too long.

A Bit O' History
After much time spent at war the owner, M'Ollark, decided to settle down for good. While travelling to the nearby city he came across the old tavern that lay in ruins near the trade route. He fell in love with it instantly and bought it the same day. After several months of hard work he reopened the tavern and since then it has become a well-known rest stop for wandering merchants and adventurers. The tavern was named after a fallen friend of M'Ollark's.

Reviews
Squikk the Bard 3/5
"Surprisingly clean establishment for such a remote village with a lot of patrons! Good food and wine, but the owner is a bit grumpy."

Krudd the Awesome 5/5
"Just perfect! Beer, food, rooms. And best of all, cheap gear!"

Fallen Knight

Description
The tavern before you appears to be an entire compound
surrounded by a stonewall and governed by a large gate. The
L-shaped two-story building within boasts a large tavern,
a stable, and a blacksmith nestled next to a small well. The
Fallen Knight echoes the nobility and refinement befitting an
establishment of its name.

A Bit O' History
Owned by a retired warrior known as Elena Langley. It has
belonged to her for several years and has developed quite the
reputation for good ale and fine food.
Recently a small gambling room has been added in which
games of chance are played. Elena herself tends to the
customers behind the bar along with her two serving girls,
Carolina and Paula. Also in her employ is a stable boy named
Jack; a maid called Jane; and Daniel, a talented cook. When
Elena is not behind the bar she can be found tending to the
forge, smithing the finest equipment in the area.

Reviews
Sardo Galato 4/5
*"There is absolutely the greatest food I have ever eaten. Also, the
rooms are clean and smell nice."*

Awis Peroko 3/5
*"Sleeping was nice and quiet. Eating was fine. Only my horse was
complaining."*

The Fat Pig

Description
Before you lies the tavern known as The Fat Pig, the worn wooden exterior sits proudly amidst this small village; albeit old, the building looks well kept. A plain wooden sign in the shape of a pig swings in the breeze above the door. You hear the grunts of pigs from behind the building muddled in with the sounds of laughter and music coming from inside the tavern.

A Bit O' History
The owner of The Fat Pig is known as 'Hog' Johnson. A man as happy as his belly is big, he runs the establishment with his tiny wife Lenna Johnson. The tavern began life as a pig farm, ran by Hog's father until Hog took over many years ago. Today Hog and his wife prepare the best pork dishes in the area for their loyal patrons. The customers are always happy, and leave well rested with smiles and full bellies.

Reviews
Father James Giles 5/5
"Hog has always taken good care of me and those that stop by the church. A warm inn and full bellies always leave everybody smiling, which warms my heart."

Jim Stoutlagger 2/5
"My Pappy could make a better pig than hog ever could! Doesn't even serve the strongest ales, only the 'popular' stuff. Bah!"

Staff and Patrons of The Fat Pig

Rick 'Hog' Johnson (Human: Bar Staff)
A tall, wide and bald man, Hog is full of smiles, laughter, and generosity. Often seen with his hands on his belly letting out a bellowing laugh, and serving drinks and food, Hog is the first to greet any newcomers to the tavern. A big belly and a bigger smile are what he's known for.

Likes: Laughter, food	Fears: Losing his inn, losing his
Dislikes: Fighting in his bar	wife
Wants: Expand his inn one day	Flaws: Loud, can't keep a secret

Lenna Johnson (Half elf: Bar Staff)
A stark contrast to Hog, Lenna is a short, slender woman. She's often seen learning on or against the bar of the Tavern. Lenna is quite the talker and loves to exchange rumours. Smiling almost as much as Hog, her long, curly, blond hair is usually pulled back while she works around the tavern.

Likes: Gossip, talking, food	Fears: Outliving her husband,
Dislikes: Dwarven food	losing the inn
Wants: Children	Flaws: Talks a lot

Father James Giles (Human: Patron)
Father Giles is a tall, slender, softly-spoken, balding old man. Retired from the military as a war priest. Often seen in his plain clothes, Giles always keeps his trusty mace 'The Disruptor' by his side, a relic of his days on the front lines.

Likes: Retirement, happiness	Fears: Being called back to
Dislikes: Violence, hate, hunger	service, memories of war
Wants: A simple life, to heal	Flaws: Cannot say no to those
the sick and feed the hungry	in need

Flying Halfling

Description
Torches either side of the door illuminate the sign that creaks above. The dark wood exterior continues into the dimly lit smoky interior of the tavern. The bar is stocked with bottles and barrels labelled with strange languages, and the fireplace in the corner draws attention to the performers that stand beside it. The kitchen produces meals solely comprised of game from the nearby forest along with various fungi grown under the tavern.

A Bit O' History
Built by a group of adventurers called "The Random Encounters", the name of the tavern originated from the group's half-orc's desire to throw their halfling friend into areas of uncertain safety. In order to commemorate the opening of the tavern, every year they still run a Halfling Tossing contest, although it is advised that halfling participation is voluntary.

Reviews
Hargan 4/5
"Since I work as a blacksmith next door I'm often here. I even got used to those strange mushrooms in the food!"

Gregor Eisenhorn 5/5
"Oh, I love this place. Not only that we serve subterranean dishes with our own planted fungi, but have you seen the door?"

Greystalk Inn

Description
The building appears recently built, the glass windows are spotless and the walls are glaringly white framed with light oak beams. An arm for a sign juts out above the door but no sign hangs there, the door is bolted shut and a piece of parchment nailed to the door reads 'Opening Soon' and 'Staff Wanted'. Through the window you see a tall lady talking to a group of bar staff.

A Bit O' History
The tavern has been newly built by Lady Greystalk, a successful tavern owner from a nearby city. The locals have been excitedly awaiting the opening of her newest tavern and many have travelled great distances to attend its opening night in a few days.

Reviews
Flaria Belltree 5/5
"Can't wait for this to open! Her other taverns are divine!"

Tomlin Hatton 1/5
"Just what we need, a load of tourists around here!"

Harbourmaster's Inn

Description
A large brickwork building stands as the cornerstone at the bottom of the creek-side village. The interior walls are painted a light pink colour and all the tables and chairs are a uniform dark oak, matching that of the bar. To the left of the main bar is a lounge, similarly decorated but with a large fireplace pressed into the wall. Paintings depicting naval battles hang on the walls and bards can be heard blasting their array of ditties in other rooms around the bar.

A Bit O' History
This simple tavern overlooks a port home to merchants from afar looking to trade goods and drink to being on dry land. The tavern used to stand as the harbourmasters abode but was lost in a game of liar's dice. The town's harbourmaster now resides on the other side of the port but the inn serves as a reminder to the luck of those in town.

Reviews
Captain Richard Roberts 4/5
"A hearty drink for the long sea ahead."

Dake Strak 3/5
"Lovely spot but overpriced as seven hells! Cannee stand the posh raff."

The Long Rest

Description
This large two-story inn and tavern have a welcoming charm that calls to the weary adventurer. From the outside, you see a wrap-around covered porch and a set of stairs that lead up to the rooms. The tavern interior boasts a very large bar with plenty of seating along its entire length. Booths line two of the walls.

A Bit O' History
Owned by an adventurer called Tevin Dow, he struck it rich and quit while he was ahead following a quest involving a dragon's hoard. Tevin spends most of the day in the kitchen while his half-elf wife, Shanis, tends to the bar and runs the staff. The staff includes the couple's two sons who run the stables; two local lasses that work as servers; and a busboy named Turpyn. Turpyn is a goblin that was freed from slavery by Tevin and now works very hard to keep the tavern spotless so is very quick to clean up any mess.

Reviews
Elandril Palish 4/5
"After surviving a treasureless, trap-filled dungeon that a wizard set up just to mess with people, The Long Rest was just what I needed. Good food and drink, comfortable beds."

Balasar Ironside 3/5
"It was good and all, but who lets a goblin run around with its head still attached?"

The Scavenging Corvus

Description
Thirsty travellers seeking refreshment hear the tavern
before they see it. The crow caws emanate from the
two-story, wooden structure. Located down a narrow street,
and surrounded by other places of business that don't
appreciate the cacophony; the space inside appears
unremarkable until visitors adjust their eyes and spy the
murder of crows vocalising from the rafters. Locals bet on
which bird will snatch up the next piece of scrap meat.

A Bit O' History
A weary magic user once visited an unremarkable tavern with
a forgotten name when a crow flew in and perched above her.
Wanting to eat her meal in peace, she enchanted the location
to prevent the crow from relieving itself within its walls. No
one's sure why the magic has lingered for so long, but the
taproom has grown in fame throughout the region. Though
the crows come and go as they please, many flock here for
food.

Reviews
Geoffry Bailey 2/5
*"While the food and drink ain't bad, the noise makes yer head hurt
long before the ale does. I don't know what's so special about a flock
of birds in a place. By the hells, if I wanted to see crows, I'd just
find myself a carcass someplace."*

The Sheaf and Scythe

Description
A simple looking building stands before you with a few obviously repaired holes in the roof. Nonetheless, it seems clean and tidy from the outside. As you venture in you are greeted by the smell of hops and fresh bread. A dozen long tables are scattered throughout the building with a space against one wall for performers to play. Against the back wall, the bar stretches across propped up by the owner, who stands waiting.

A Bit O' History
Known in the local area as a producer of some of the best bread available, people often come here just for a chunk of their famous farmhouse loaf. Fred is the human, middle-aged barman with fading hair, a light-brown beard, and a large belly. Sitting on a crossroads in a village, many adventurers pass through this area and can occasionally compete with each other on war stories and tales of heroism.

Reviews
Malcer 3/5
"It's a little bit of a walk from my farm, but the ale is fresh, the bread is warm and the people are friendly."

Lob 3/5
"Reasonable prices, decent food, good atmosphere but can be a bit rough."

Staff and Patrons of The Sheaf and Scythe

Karsa Orlong (Mountain dwarf: Patron)

At over three feet wide and bare-chested, Karsa is an eye-catching sight. A bear claw hangs around his neck, and five white scars trace across his chest. In spite of all this Karsa's hair and beard are well groomed and oiled.

Likes: Ale, the chance for glory	Fears: He will not meet expectations
Dislikes: Indecisive people	
Wants: To find who destroyed his hometown	Flaws: His pride

Flint (Half demon: Patron)

Shrouded in a large robe that covers most of the face, it is hard to tell Flint is anything but human. Dark tanned skin with a quarterstaff at his side, he sits in a dark corner alone with his head bowed and fingers interlaced. A plate of food sits in front of him, untouched as he sits looking pensive.

Likes: Order and balance	Fears: What his past may contain, persecution
Dislikes: Fiends, devils, and people who exploit others	
Wants: Information on his past	Flaws: He is rigid in his way of thinking

Malcer Lackman (Human: Patron)

A local man who works the land, with calloused hands, tanned skin and sandy hair. He has a few days of stubble and appears flustered, moving from person to person asking them for help.

Likes: Quiet life, crops	Fears: That he never did enough with his life
Dislikes: Rats, confrontation	
Wants: Someone to help get rid of the rat problem at the farm	Flaws: Underexposed to the world outside his farmstead

A Stone's Throw

Description

A heavy stone building, this tavern is rugged in construction though visually plain. Those who are versed in such things will notice the quality and practicality of this building, which must be centuries old. A warm hearth greets weary traders and adventurers, offering protection from the cold winds outside. Various rugs line the stone floor, and tables and chairs circle the area around the hearth. The tavern offers hearty mugs of ale and cider, while the kitchen serves home-style meals, using fresh produce from the surrounding farms.

A Bit O' History

Originally built by dwarves, this building was converted into an inn centuries ago. Its heavy walls and sturdy construction tell the story of dwarves eager to strike out into the world, shunning their insular cousins and engaging with the world around them.

Reviews

Grunt, The People's Champion 5/5

"Now this is the kind of place Grunt could get used to! Loud, crowded and the ale flows all night long! The People's Champion approves!"

Maximillion Moonberry 2/5

"Though fine a place as any to rest my tired halfling feet, the acoustics of this establishment are entirely unsuitable for performance."

Travellers Rest

Description
The half-timber tavern sits beside an old barn, which now
functions as a stable and guest accommodation and appears
connected to the tavern by a covered bridge. The thick
stonewalls and small windows allow for little light as you
enter the tavern proper. The glow of candlelight flickers
around the tables that populate the main floor, while the
staircase to the left leads up to a balcony that runs along to
the adjoining barn. The barman smiles as you enter.

A Bit O' History
Situated next to a small river, what was once a solitary
building soon became an entire village. For reasons unknown
a fire consumed the tavern one day, and the villagers helped
recover what they could and moved it next to an old barn
nearby. The tavern has been run by the same family for four
generations and is greatly respected and adored by the locals.

Reviews
Cormak 3/5
*"I come here quite often, I like the cosy bar area. The rooms are
minimalist, but I don't need much."*

Lecyll 2/5
*"I had to stay here for three nights. I had a good room but the
tavern was hosting a group of dwarves, it was quite noisy."*

Wayfarer's Rest

Description

The Wayfarer's Rest is a wood-framed, three-story building with a long wing of two stories extending from its side. Stables and a fenced yard can be seen beyond, ensuring the relatively new structure appears far too large for the village, which can surely only be home to a couple of hundred souls. Nevertheless, there appears to be quite a crowd in and around the building, even at this modest hour.

A Bit O' History

The Wayfarer's Rest began simply as the humble village inn and tavern. This all changed when Turold became the innkeeper and fortuitously hired an outstanding brewmaster. Even though most trade goes via the main road, once word of the excellent room and board became known, many merchants and caravans started going out of their way along the Forest Road just to stay for the night. Their beer is unrivalled!

Reviews

Tungem the Rotund 5/5
"Best beer in the region!"

Rosiv Applecart 3/5
"Too crowded! I liked the old inn better."

Staff and Patrons of Wayfarer's Rest

Turold (Human: Innkeeper)

Turold is a pleasant, if nondescript, man of early middle age. Standing at average height with brown hair and hazel eyes, he seems to be constantly in motion. His wife Vella and daughter Xella are never far, helping to shoulder his responsibilities.

Likes: Great food and drink Dislikes: Dishonesty Wants: To get things running smoothly!	Fears: Being in over his head Flaws: Biting off more than he can chew

Lyssa (Human: Server)

Lyssa is a local girl of nineteen. Slim of build and startlingly good looking. Happy to use her looks to her advantage she is mercilessly flirtatious, but her male patrons don't mind when she turns her intense green eyes their way.

Likes: Being the centre of attention. Dislikes: Intense relationships. Wants: To be more than a serving wench	Fears: Being tied down Flaws: She is not always the best judge of character

Merrin (Human: Brewmaster)

Merrin is a man in his early thirties with blonde hair, blue eyes, and pale skin. He stands only five feet five inches tall. Quiet and reserved, though not unfriendly, he is a hard person to get talking unless it is about brewing.

Likes: Peace and quiet Dislikes: Crowds Wants: A separate brewery	Fears: Being centre of attention Flaws: He doesn't say what he really thinks

Wilderness
Taverns

Places of refuge are few and far between in the wilderness, as such we found the prices to be somewhat inflated. Many establishments welcomed strangers whereas others looked upon us as though we were trespassing; it seems that a few proprietors count on not being easily found and therefore run a more, private service. Look under every rock and leave no leaf unturned, many places may be more hidden than you expected.

Adventurer's Rest

Description
Between the trees, you see a three-story building made entirely of dark mahogany. The entrance appears guarded by two large, well built human males that give you a cursory nod as you enter. Set out over a number of floors, everything from merchants to a skilled smithy is available to all those that have gained a full membership. Guest patrons are granted basic amenities, but you may want to visit the contract board and complete a quest or two in order to gain access to the exclusive services found on the upper floors.

A Bit O' History
The tavern was created by a group called The Dragon's Talon. The idea was to create a place for adventurers to come together and relax, whilst also giving them the opportunity to find work. The Tavern is currently run by the last surviving member of the Dragon's Talon called Master Vestus, a silver dragon in human form, though only club members know this.

Reviews
Lester Firebeard 5/5
"Adventurer's Rest is expensive, but is worth every gold piece!"

Rufus Hallow 4/5
"Adventurer's Rest is the best tavern I've ever been to. Unfortunately, it burns a hole in my pocket."

The Banished Inn

Description
The Banished Inn sits within a wooden palisade guarded by a large orc at the gate. The main building stands three stories tall and the stables stand in its shadow. Given the appearance of the buildings, they have clearly been here for a number of years. The simple interior of the inn is large and welcoming with a clean and warm atmosphere that smells of pine.

A Bit O' History
The inn was born out of a forbidden love between an Orc and a dwarven female during a time of war. Both were banished from their respective tribes and were sent into isolation.
The Inn now stands as a testament to their love and resolve to do what their hearts desired. The dwarven female runs the bar and kitchen with a small amount of staff and her husband stands guard and keeps the peace. The Inn does not tolerate violence or prejudice against the varying races that visit.

Reviews
Gkod Stonedeath 4/5
"It was nice to have a tavern where we could drink the good stuff. The smell of the dwarves was a bit distracting"

Anugteig Firerider 2/5
"A smelly tavern filled with uncivilized folk. The only good thing was that they were in the middle of a forest I didn't want to sleep under the sky."

Birchwood Keep

Description
Birchwood Keep is located in the heart of the forest. There are only two ways to access it. Those that know how to navigate through the secret woods using a very specific set of instructions, or those that call on the help of the Jester (the owners familiar). Shortly after you call for Jester he will arrive very inconspicuously and the wise traveler will know to follow him to a place of respite.

A Bit O' History
Leaph went through a lot of trouble to make sure he was not troubled with the riff-raff that you would normally find amongst normal taverns.

No wenches or waiters. Just the owner and his pet.

Reviews
Leaph 5/5
"Since very few travellers know about this tavern it is very exclusive and only the shadows of those worthy enough to darken its doorway find their way to Birchwood Keep."

Borrow 2/5
"The food and drink were not to my liking, but it was secluded enough that I was not bothered"

The Castaway

Description
A large two-storied tavern on the shore of a huge lake. The
building appears in good condition with a sign hanging above
the door which reads, "The Castaway" sitting proudly over
an image of a rope and anchor. A large dock extends out into
the lake behind the tavern with numerous boats moored to it.
Music and laughter can be heard coming from inside. Smoke
spirals from multiple chimneys as you cheerfully eye this
happy looking tavern, you then catch a glimpse of a shady
figure stepping away from a window on the upper floor.

A Bit O' History
The castaway caters to fisherman, woodsmen, and people
of means who have estates on or around the lake. There is a
bar area split by a small stage where Stephen the bard plays
and a dining area with half a dozen large tables. Jodar and
his girlfriend Rosie Wishwalla own and run the place; they
are usually open late long into the night. They have a room
upstairs for rent although it usually goes unoccupied as it is
rumored to be haunted.

Reviews
Edmund Grundvar, Owner of Lumber Consortium 5/5
*"We go to the Castaway a couple nights a week. Jodar is a great
bartender and keeps us well entertained with jokes and tales.
It is great fun and the braised lamb with sweet potatoes is amazing!
But I could swear I heard someone yelling upstairs."*

Chirpy Oak

Description
The giant oak tree dwarfs its competition in the great forest.
Blue light from the lamps call out from the hollowed out tree.
Inside, similar blue lanterns hang from an ornately carved
ceiling, creating a wonderfully calm and almost seductive
atmosphere. Its engraved interior, polished bar, and tidy
upkeep make it stand out from all other taverns you have seen
in the wilderness. A huge stage carved from the tree sits on
the far right of the entrance and a huge staircase leads
towards the upper bedrooms and storehouse.

A Bit O' History
The gatepost of an Elven city, travellers would have stayed
here before being permitted entry into the heart of the city.
As the years passed, war ravaged the land and the city was
eventually sacked and fell victim to ruin, but the gatepost
remained and slowly became more of a meeting place for all
sorts of adventurers on the road. Its upkeep was maintained
by three Elven brothers who then started to play host to the
many bards and poets that graced the wilderness.

Reviews
Nixxy Ricks 4/5
*"Wonderful songs and beautiful ballads. I would stay here if I
could."*

The Crone's Nest

Description

The Crone's Nest is a rambling assortment of awnings and lean-tos surrounding a massive galleon that was shipwrecked during a violent maelstrom. It appears severely battle damaged with many cannon marks and holes in the sides. The bleached remains of a hag are lashed to the crow's nest of the mast, presumably lending the tavern its name. The ship leans slightly to one side so the interior is a touch disorientating, however, the tables and lightning are very pleasing to the eye. Behind the bar is a wide assortment of drinks, as well as suspicious bottles of potions and poisons in a myriad of lurid colours. The barkeep is an ancient, crumpled looking woman. Merchants can be found doing, often shady, business in the encampment, along with disguised nobles looking for rookie adventurers to go on dangerous quests.

Reviews

Ixtoan Revark 5/5

"The exterior is somewhat lacking but once inside the furnishings are surprisingly plush, and the food and wine prepared were truly exquisite as were the lodgings. The clientele are a tad suspicious but I suppose you take what you can when being off the beaten path. I shall surely return."

Barathin Boddynock 1/5

"Ay smelt Magyck on tha aer and after ay dispelled it ay can safely say ay nair wish ta return to this vile hovel of lies."

First Quest Tavern

Description
Within a goblin-ridden cavern near a goblin-plagued town stands a lone bar surrounded by benches and stools. Though this part of the cave is well lit and goblin-free, the sounds of nearby flesh hungry vermin do not escape your ears. The bar is busy with fresh-faced adventurers and wounded allies preparing, and commiserating, respectively. The staff appear to be well equipped and experienced adventurers that pay no mind to the environment they find themselves in. Ale and healing potions seem to be flowing in equal measure.

A Bit O' History
The tavern was set up by a group of well-travelled adventurers that wanted to support the development of their craft: adventuring. By setting up a business in a popular spot for first-time adventurers they enjoy a steady flow of customers and the support of the local town. By enlisting adventurers to complete small quests they help keep the nearby village free of goblins, therefore becoming very popular in the area. Though sometimes goblins stray into their area of the cave they are no match for the proprietors of the establishment.

Reviews
Ignaris Spellblade 3/5
"Great for first-time adventurers, a bit dull for those with more experience."

Green Goblet Sanctuary

Description
Only guides and forest folk know of this tavern's existence, although some adventurers have come to hear of it. The building appears to have been built with an eclectic fusion of styles. The food is average, the company is strange, but the peace inside is absolute. The large building has plenty of rooms to offer and music plays near continuously.

A Bit O' History
Once run by the mighty giant slayer, Garoum, whose two-handed sword still hangs by the fire, the Inn has become a haven of peace in the wake of a violent past. The tavern is now run by Garoums widow, Tanasha, and their two sons. Regular patrons tend to be forest folk and fey creatures. The food is nothing special, but it is a relaxing place to meet strangers. Some adventurers have spoken of a gateway of sorts in the area, though many cannot recall any details.

Reviews
Doran Clank, the woodcutter 5/5
"I was sure I would die after running away from that beast that attacked me. I ran all night and was nearly frozen to death when I saw the tavern. Now – I come here all the time."

Alathillal Oennen, Prince of Elvendom 3/5
"The place has seen better days, they let any human riff-raff in! It is no longer a place for the forest-folk and I only go on business these days."

Hammer Twins Inn

Description
As you enter the wide clearing you see a solid, bluestone building that looks more like a stronghold than a cosy inn. As you enter, you see dark-wood floors, and walls partially covered in thick rugs and tapestries. A roaring fireplace sits at one end of the room, and a general hum of conversation fills the air. You are immediately hit with the smell of roasting meats, baking bread and an array of spices and herbs. It speaks of comfort amid a harsh environment.

A Bit O' History
Designed and built by former adventurers, the Hammer Twins is a way station for adventurers, used as a means of resting either on the way to a dangerous locale or as a respite on the way back to civilization from an adventure. Constructed with Dwarven stonework and the best arcane improvements gold can buy, this inn is a formidable stronghold for those resting inside.

Reviews
Elwyn Fayenote 3/5
"While the food and wine were acceptable, there was a dearth of live music and I wasn't allowed to remedy this!"

Garshnuk 5/5
"Good foods, strong ales, no women but still had fun!"

93

Staff and Patrons of Hammer Twins Inn

Korda Und (Mountain dwarf: Owner)

Despite her stature, Korda is an intimidating dwarf with thick muscles, plenty of scars and no hair to be seen. She gives patrons a genuinely warm smile as they enter and ushers them to a table. She moves with a warrior's grace and seems absolutely in command of everything around her at all times.

Likes: Battle, treasure, mead	Fears: Losing her sister
Dislikes: Dishonesty, cowards	Flaws: Believes she's not
Wants: Peaceful retirement	vulnerable, rushes into battle

Vanyali Und (Mountain dwarf: Owner)

Bearing a striking resemblane to her sister, Korda, the only real difference between them is Vanyali's lack of musculature. Vanyali is often approached by those seeking knowledge and wisdom.

Likes: Arcane lore, women,	Fears: Losing her sister
wine	Flaws: Looks down on those
Dislikes: Orcs, dishonesty,	who don't understand magic
abuse of arcane power	
Wants: Peaceful retirement	

Tinu Nenar (High elf: Waiter)

A tall lithe elf, with long straight hair the colour of the midnight sky, his beauty might have once turned heads. Now they turn away from a hideous burn that covers three-quarters of his face, though this hasn't lessened his arrogance or ego.

Likes: Women, song	Fears: His scars, poverty
Dislikes: Work of any kind	Flaws: Arrogance, pride,
Wants: Respect, power, wealth	xenophobia

Hull and Breach

Description
Nestled in the northern mountains, it is one of the strangest sites in the world. The hull of an upturned ship sits hundreds of miles from any coast. A fire burns in the middle of the taproom surrounded by chairs and tables; two lengthy bars line either side, the left, boasting an array of spirits and the right, kegs, and ales. Though slightly disorientating, the many decks are still used for guest rooms and a large basement has been carved out to accommodate a large stonewalled kitchen.

A Bit O' History
Hidden away amongst the snow-capped mountain villages, the Hull and Breach's origins remain a mystery. Initially used as a stronghold populated by a gang of barbarians it later became a meeting place for miners, which turned rapidly into a tavern. Its patrons are mainly dwarves from the local mining towns and adventurers wandering in search of treasures buried beneath the mountain.

Reviews
Tyron Two-Hands 4/5
"An adventurers haven in the middle of the goddamn nowhere!"

Don Jerew 3/5
"It's a nice spot but the location's too cold and I was sat next to a barbarian! The humanity!"

Lady Luna's Sports Tavern

Description
The tavern is made of strong sturdy wood, covered with vines that grow throughout the building. The furnishings appear to have grown from the very forest the tavern resides in. Adorned with many trophies from the travels of Luna and Lontari the spacious tavern provides ample space for crowds of patrons. On the far side of the tavern, beyond the long bar, a large area is reserved for various sporting events.

A Bit O' History
It was once the home of two adventurers, Luna Thunderpaw and Lontari Al'Agrios. After many adventures, they decided to settle down and turn their home into a place where adventurers could rest, get information and test their skill against each other. What began as Lontari challenging visitors to friendly competitions has become a series of celebrated tournaments. Though Luna and Lontari gave up adventuring they still act as the guardians of the forest, using the tavern to keep an eye on those who pass through.

Reviews
Feng the Malice 5/5
"The swordsmanship of the dark elf that lives in the tavern was worth the travel alone!"

Sin Grimfoot 5/5
"Owned by a truly enchanting woman. The entertainment was fascinating, and they allowed me to sell some of my wares here."

Staff and Patrons of Lady Luna's Sports Tavern

Lontari Al'Agrios (Dark elf: Owner/ Ranger)

Lontari is an imposing, black-skinned drow with a lean muscular build and bright red eyes that burn with passion for competition. His long white hair is unkempt and covers more than half of his back. He keeps a scimitar with a glowing crimson hilt on his hip, which gives off steam as if it is heating the air around it. He wears hand wraps that barely cover the violet runes engraved on his skin. Lontari runs the tavern with his wife Luna.

Likes: Competing with worthy adventurers Dislikes: Rich, snobby people and losing Wants: To allow travellers to test their skill in competition	Fears: That his skin colour will force out worthy adventurers Flaws: Strong adventurers get him overexcited

Luna Thunderpaw (Moon elf: Bar Owner)

Luna is the most beautiful woman of the Wildwoods. She has delicate, light-bluish hued skin and big, bright-blue eyes. Wavy light-green hair falls down her back, with the left-side in two braids, intertwined with the feathers of her ancestors. Luna is slim, with light muscle tone. Brown and grey feathers dress Luna's arms suggesting her strong ties to the druidic arts. A silver claw-shaped pendant emits a glow from her neck.

Likes: Running through the forest in her many beast forms Dislikes: Those who disrespect nature Wants: To keep the peace of the forest	Fears: The forest being inhabited by too many outsiders Flaws: Overprotective of nature that causes her to act rash in certain situations

The Lair

Description

While the name of the bar and its exterior appearance may well change, Nox, and his two permanent staff, Hikaru and Kaoru, stay the same. Nox's tavern seems to change location as the need arises, and has been known to be found in other planes of existence. Nox appears to be your average barkeep but he has much information to sell, for the right price. The tavern is clean and well maintained, although the decor is somewhat off-putting to some. There seems to be many shady corners for all manner of business.

A Bit O' History

Nox runs the tavern, aided by "The Twins". He is a tall, thin man with untidy black hair and deep-red eyes. He is often sarcastic or derisive to his customers, almost as if he is impatiently awaiting his true calling, but will always help people new to the area, even to his own detriment. The Twins are his bar-staff and bouncers.

Reviews

The Alabaster Mask 5/5

"Always here when I need it, with good drink. People know I'm here to find a hire so it works for me."

Rancid the Ribald Goblin 3/5

"It's alright, innit? Though the guy running this'un's a bit freaky, as are those twins. Always grinning! It's always clean and tidy if a bit dark but the prices ain't bad."

Staff and Patrons of The Lair

Nox (Vampire: Owner/ Intelligence Broker)
Nox is a particularly tall, thin man with untidy black hair, deep-red eyes and looks to be in his mid-thirties. He constantly wears a blank, disinterested expression and can't seem to get through a sentence without being sarcastic.

Likes: Decorating, colourful cocktails Dislikes: Cleaning, daytime Wants: Better servants	Fears: Not being needed Flaws: Overly supportive, even to his own detriment

Hikaru and Kaoru (Human spirits: Bouncers/ Waiters)
Identical twins in their late teens, they stand out in any crowd for their perfect hair, stunning looks, and impeccable fashion sense. They share an almost constant mischievous grin and a fitting sense of mischief.

Likes: Each other Dislikes: Not getting attention Wants: People who will treat them as individuals	Fears: Nox, being separated Flaws: They crave attention and will push boundaries to get it

The Alabaster Mask (Unknown: Patron)
The man at the bar always wears a white alabaster mask. He's come here for years and has never changed, or maybe he changes every time? He'll be your mercenary, your information gatherer and your hired hand, whatever you need of him. One thing stays constant, however: he's an enigma.

Likes: Having something to do Dislikes: Talking, anyone trying to take his mask off Wants: To be kept busy	Fears: Nox's wrath Flaws: Likes his liquor

The Legions Rest

Description

You spot a well maintained tavern situated atop a hill surrounded by trees a short distance from the trade roads. Comprised of several buildings that house a stable, a fletcher, storerooms and the tavern itself with rooms to rent. The ever burning hearth welcomes weary travellers from afar accompanied by the sounds of travelling bards and the various forms of entertainment that you can take part in. Laughter and revelry echoes around the buildings as knives are thrown, arrows are drawn, and lutes played.

A Bit O' History

Run by a married couple that were once adventurers. They keep things running smoothly with a small number of staff; along with their incredibly talented daughter who runs the forge and their son who is both an elven trained fletcher and stablemaster. Being experienced adventurers, signs of violence or aggression outside the wrestling ring and other forms of entertainment are dealt with swiftly and cleanly.

Reviews

Straight SilverArrow 5/5
"Bright, warm, ideally situated for basic supplies and swift repairs and they take good care of your animals."

Ricross Battlebeard 3/5
"The barkeep stocks a great selection of ales but it's a bit too clean inside."

Skellars

Description

Nestled within the thick trees and gloomy light, a dark wood building stands mute in the stillness. The broken and weathered shack does nothing to welcome visitors, save for the light of a single lantern that dwindles in the darkness. The locals would tell you it is an abandoned hideout for an old criminal, but the locals lie. If you wait long enough many people come and go, leaving in various states of inebriation accompanied by song and revelry.

A Bit O' History

The hideout belonged to one of the most notorious criminals in history; though long dead, he avoided capture until he died of old age. With the help of a powerful wizard, an illusory ward was placed over the area. Without the key, Skellars will appear as an abandoned shelter, forever to be lost in the gloom. Over the years many keys were made, most of these small amulets lay in the possession of the new owners, though some remain lost. A well-kept secret among the locals, beyond the illusion Skellars is a wondrously lavish mansion.

Reviews

Breen 0/5
"Skellars? I've heard of it yes, can't say that I've ever been there though..."

Yellow Lantern

Description
Whether rounding the corner of the darkest dungeon or
braving the depths of the deep forests, if you see the warm
glow of a single yellow lantern you can breathe a sigh of
relief. The single lantern hangs from a pole attached to a
ramshackle cart, accompanied by a strange fellow that greets
you with a toothless grin. Though you may find yourself in
the worst of situations the warm glow is comforting. The
crooked, humanoid figure brings out a couple of brown,
unlabelled bottles from his cart and beckons you forward.

A Bit O' History
Not many people know of this strange tavern if you could
call it one. Found in the strangest of places, the kind old
man is always happy to help adventurers find what they need.
Fiercely disciplined in the arcane arts, his solitary travels are
of no concern to him. If asked why he travels, he says he is
looking for something, but he cannot recall what.

Reviews
Brent Youngling 5/5
*"I don't know what I would have done without the old mage. We
had just run out of potions."*

Lord Pontice 1/5
*"You are seriously calling that beggars cart a tavern? My dear boy,
you need to travel more."*

Vinewood Teahouse

Description
Amidst the sounds of birds and swaying trees, the leaf-covered tavern appears to have grown from the forest floor itself. Made of intertwined vines and leaves, this tavern celebrates its surroundings and the wood elves that built it. The tavern is formed of several pods and canopies that give plenty of privacy to those that wish to drink their tea, and smoke their pipes, in peace.

A Bit O' History
Built by three wood-elves that once lived in a busy city, they returned to the forest and built the teahouse for a more peaceful version of what they had experienced in traditional taverns. Though no ale or meat is served here, a range of intoxicating teas, flavoured tobacco, and strange herbal delicacies can be purchased here which produce similar effects.

Reviews
Ki'tori Mallion 4/5
"Delightfully relaxing, it was nice to attune with nature once more."

Feylun Gnimley 5/5
"Wow! What a magnificent place! Try the bottlebug tea!"

Wrong Question

Description
Walking through the door you see a clean, plain and pleasant bar with a sparring ring on one side, and a dojo on the other. The vast majority of the patrons are meditating or watching the combat intently, it is unnervingly quiet. Over the Bar, there is a large Golden plaque declaring "Show me how you FIGHT, and I will tell you WHO you are." Behind the Bar is a kindly looking older man, who greets you cheerfully, "What'll it be?"

A Bit O' History
One of the last sites where Martial Cognition is practiced, the proprietor, Master Do, can read ones essence to provide holistic knowledge and Precognitive Oracles, on one condition: if this is your first night at "The Wrong Question" you have to fight. Cost is determined fairly after the reading, so you better bring enough or you'll be indentured for some time. Rumour has it "The Wrong Question" exists in flux appearing where and when it is needed.

Reviews
Kassandra Mileh 5/5
"What does it mean to be? Is the Wrong Question!"

Phil the Rube 1/5
"I just wanted to be a ninja and instead I'm stuck here an indentured servant, I'm never going to learn anything about fighting because I'm always working."

104

Cellars and Secrets

Taverns and inns usually have a perpetual flow of strangers through their doors. Though they may have their regulars, it's easy to understand how some innkeepers and barkeeps can cover up any secrets without notice. Whether it's hiding something from their patrons - or simply misleading their customers so they don't see what's really going on - some of these taverns are hiding something.

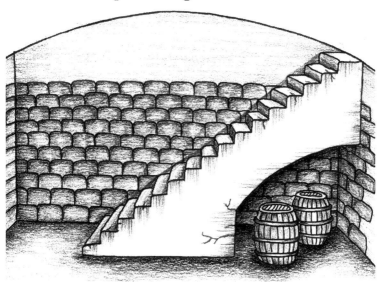

Secrets - D6

1	Hidden room
2	Secret tunnel
3	It's all a front
4	Something's not right
5	A private section
6	Hidden cellar/ basement

Hidden room - D4

A hidden room may not be as ominous as it seems. But if it's hidden, it's got to be hidden for a reason. These rooms could be found anywhere, from behind a simple door in the kitchens to a secret entrance that looks like a hearth. Proprietors often do whatever it takes to keep their hidden rooms a secret.

1	Used for gambling
2	As a meeting room
3	As a refuge
4	Used for hiding contraband

Secret tunnel - D6

On occasion, secret tunnels have sat dormant without even the barkeep's knowledge. Sometimes they sit as remnants of a previously trying time, demonstrating the resilience and rebellious nature of the prior populace. In any case, a secret tunnel often leads to somewhere of consequence.

1	Out of the city/town/village/area
2	To a brewery
3	To a safehouse
4	To another tavern
5	To a dungeon
6	To a shrine

It's all a front - D4

The light-hearted and jovial atmosphere you enjoy in your local tavern may not be as it seems. Sometimes if you scratch the surface you start to see things differently. The business and its staff may be there to cover up something else the building is used for, perhaps a faction or guild.

1	For the local thieves guild
2	For a smuggling operation
3	For a group of heroes laying low
4	For a cult

Something's not right - D6

You may not know what it is, but sometimes something just doesn't feel right. That nagging feeling in your gut that tugs at the mind as you gaze upon this otherwise normal looking scene - these are the kind of secrets that could leave people in deep trouble and lead them down paths that they cannot undo.

1	Strange noises coming from the basement
2	People have been going missing
3	The barkeep looks...strange
4	The food tastes really odd
5	The staff have suddenly changed
6	People don't look like they want to be here

A private section - D4

Not all secrets are malicious but that doesn't mean you aren't interested in what's going on. Some taverns have private sections away from the regular crowds designed for entrance only given certain permissions.

1	For members only
2	For VIPs
3	For private functions
4	That is set up for an event happening soon

Hidden cellar/ basement - D8

The life of a tavern owner or innkeeper can be a difficult one; often they are subjected to all manner of misgivings and foul play. As a result, some have resorted to hiding things or storing goods away from prying eyes. That's not to say that they are always hiding things of a savoury nature.

1	Full of stolen goods
2	Packed full of vintage spirits and ales
3	It's been emptied but recently
4	Full of old adventuring equipment and trophies
5	It's an interrogation room or a torture chamber
6	It's full of scrolls and old tomes
7	It looks like some sort of laboratory
8	It's a prison

Drinks and Distractions

Create Your Own: Beers, Wines and Spirits

Taverns, bars, pubs, and inns - call them what you will but they all have one thing in common, they are stocked with drink. Ales, wines, spirits, and beers, whatever your tipple, these establishments are sure to quench any thirst or desire. Where do these drinks come from, however?

Usually, the house ale is brewed on site, as the name suggests, but what about the rest of the menu? What other products do other breweries, distilleries, and wine houses produce that encourage the patrons to stay for a while?

Over the next few pages you will find a set of tables that will help you answer these questions.

Beers and Ales

D20	Part One	D20	Part Two
1	Drunken	1	Pirate
2	Noble	2	Goblin
3	Whimpering	3	Wench
4	Drooling	4	Prince
5	Proud	5	Lord
6	Penniless	6	Dwarf
7	Gilded	7	Bandit
8	Shaking	8	Priest
9	Glistening	9	Lich
10	Sneaky	10	Assassin
11	Wishful	11	Queen
12	Glamourous	12	Witch
13	Filthy	13	King
14	Jumping	14	Farmer
15	Kinky	15	Sailor
16	Greedy	16	Orc
17	Belching	17	Damsel
18	Orphaned	18	Princess
19	Sleeping	19	Thief
20	Hanging	20	Hero

Fine Wines, Spirits and Liquors

D20	Part One	D20	Part Two
1	Witches	1	Plight
2	Maidens	2	Tools
3	Adventurers	3	Tipple
4	Dwarves	4	Quest
5	Farmers	5	Coin Purse
6	Knights	6	Reserve
7	Druids	7	Tonic
8	Kings	8	Potion
9	Thieves	9	Downfall
10	Goblins	10	Courage
11	Smithys	11	Collection
12	Warriors	12	Hoard
13	Peasants	13	Special
14	Bards	14	Choice
15	Dragons	15	Poison
16	Orcs	16	Contract
17	Devils	17	Cask
18	Mummers	18	Work
19	Gods	19	Reward
20	Lords	20	Gift

How does it taste?

D20	It tastes...	D20	With a ... finish
1	Smooth	1	Chocolaty
2	Watery	2	Buttery
3	Bitter	3	Sticky
4	Velvety	4	Crisp
5	Sour	5	Interesting
6	Fragrant	6	Strange
7	Harsh	7	Floral
8	Silky	8	Fine
9	Tangy	9	Bubbly
10	Peppery	10	Light
11	Oaky	11	Undrinkable
12	Leathery	12	Flat
13	Foul	13	Cheeky
14	Strange	14	Chalky
15	Fruity	15	Complex
16	Firey	16	Salty
17	Bold	17	Indescribable
18	Spicy	18	Lingering
19	Refreshing	19	Chewy
20	Refined	20	Flawless

D20 - Tavern Distraction

D20	Distraction/ Situation
1	Someone yells, "drinks on me"
2	A cup smashes on the floor behind the bar
3	Some city guards walk in
4	There's something going on outside
5	Someone has been murdered
6	The tavern erupts into song
7	A patron is kicked out
8	A shady looking character appears
9	Enthralled by song
10	Out of beer
11	Everybody out
12	Your purchase cost more than expected
13	You're unwelcome
14	It all began in a tavern
15	Too drunk to care
16	A quiet drink
17	That escalated quickly
18	Such generosity
19	Mistaken identity
20	Master brew

1. Someone yells, 'Drinks are on me!'
The tavern becomes a hive of commotion, people from all corners of the room scurry to the bar to claim their free drinks. Drinks are spilled, people are ripped from their seats by the tide of patrons, and it is chaos!

2. A cup smashes on the floor behind the bar!
The entire room of patrons cheers in chorus and raise their cups in laughter! The mixture of abashed bar staff and rowdy patrons make for the perfect diversion for opportunists.

3. Some city guards walk in!
Obviously out of place, two members of the city guard enter the tavern. The noise falls to a quizzical silence, save for a few hushed voices. They approach the barkeep and show them a piece of parchment with someone's face drawn upon it.

4. There's something going on outside!
Amidst the revelry and joyous atmosphere within the tavern, a voice breaks out over the drone of patrons. "There's something going on out there!" they cry as they peak out the steamy glass. Some of the patrons rush to get a glimpse.

5. Someone had been murdered!
Despite numerous possible witnesses, a body is found and the murderer could be someone within the tavern!

6. The tavern erupts into song!
Whether accompanied by music or not, the locals of the area have long since enjoyed a rousing song that has been passed down through the generations. The unified voice of those in the tavern is deafening but you are hard pressed not to feel uplifted by the spirits of those you drink with!

7. A patron is kicked out!

A considerably inebriated patron is dragged across the tavern by the scruff of the neck and thrown clean through the doors. Do they look familiar?

8. A shady looking character appears!

No one else seems to notice the cloaked figure entering the tavern. They slink across the bar area and take a seat in the corner. The figure's hood lifts slightly and you think you see thin smile as you continue to stare but a passing patron breaks your vision. You look back to find the figure has gone.

9. Enthralled by song!

The bard starts playing and the tavern is full of patrons now sitting in silence, focused upon the music of the bard in the corner. Tears glisten in the eyes of the patrons and bar staff during this moving performance. Anyone in the tavern will instantly hush any noise that attempts to draw his or her attention from the bard.

10. Out of beer!

The tavern has minimal supplies after many busy nights but the barkeep is doing all that they can to keep patrons drinking what they have left.

11. Everybody out!

For reasons unknown the barkeep calls the tavern to a close and begins ushering patrons out.

12. Your purchase cost more than expected!

At some point during the night, you lost something. Only when you realise something is missing do you remember someone bumping into you a little too intentionally.

13. You're unwelcome!

From the moment you entered the tavern you've felt uneasy as if you're being watched. Everyone in the tavern is studying your actions and interactions. Any requests you make of the bar staff is met with scepticism and disdain.

14. It all began in a tavern!

A ragtag bunch of young looking would-be adventurers stumble through the doors of the tavern. They fumble with their weapons and straighten their clothes, which appear ill-fitting and mismatched. One of the group steps forwards. He clears his throat and announces, "We are here for the quest!" after which he proudly places his clenched fists on his hips and raises his chin smugly. The group is met with roaring laughter after a stunned silence.

15. Too drunk to care!

It has been a long day and is set to be an even longer night. The patrons seem to have indulged a little too much and the bar staff aren't much better. You might ask of the occasion (if any) but no sense can be drawn from these drunken fools.

16. A quiet drink?

Without warning, every patron within the tavern walks calmly to the nearest exit. The barkeep moves to start flipping the chairs and stools onto the tables and begins their duties for closing for the evening. Despite all this, you are more than welcome to stay and have a quiet drink in the corner while the staff clean up.

17. That escalated quickly!

At some point during the night, someone stands and yells at another patron. A fight breaks out between them and before you know it, the entire bar erupts into a vicious brawl. No piece of furniture or glassware is safe.

18. Such generosity!

A human man climbs up onto the bar above the crowd of patrons next to you. He flashes you a cheeky smile and a wink and looks to the attentive gathering of patrons.
"Ladies and Gents!" he calls, "The drinks are on this kind soul right here!" as he gestures in your direction. The crowd cheers and you find yourself surrounded by grateful patrons, as the bar is flooded with those looking to acquire their free drink.

19. Mistaken identity!

A large, heavyset man covered in scars approaches you. He looks cautiously before saying; "So I hear you are the one that can get the job done?" He nods expectantly at you and, before you can respond, he places a small bag of coins in your hand and whispers, "If it's not done properly, I'll find you!" He stands and leaves.

20. Master brew!

The tavern's atmosphere feels unusually upbeat and excitable. It turns out there is a famous Master brewer in town and he brings with him one of his specialty ales! Everyone is eager to try some and everyone knows he's only here for the night before he moves on to the next town!

Tavern Games

In this section, you will find a number of games that you might come across when visiting a tavern. Games, contests, and gambling are commonplace in most establishments.

Most proprietors consider it another form of entertainment that they offer. Some barkeeps may openly advertise games whereas others, given local laws, may run secret ones for a chosen few.

Beggars Blackjack

Beggars Blackjack is a gambling game for 3 or more players. The aim of the game is to be the player with the closest value to 21, using your dice plus one from another player. To begin the game all the players place the entry fee in the middle, players then roll 3d6 in secret before moving on to the betting phase.

In a clockwise rotation players take it in turns to either raise the bet, forfeit their stake, or pass the play onto the next player (if the bet has not been raised). If two or more players remain after this stage they move onto the final phase of the game; if only one remains, that player takes the pot.

In the final stage, before everyone's values are revealed, each of the active players must select another player to beg a dice from. The players may choose someone that folded in the previous round of betting, they may all choose the same person and may choose the same dice value when the dice are revealed.

The final score is the total of the players own dice, plus one dice value from their selected player. The score closest to 21 without going over wins. Active players split the pot evenly in the event of a draw and if everyone busts (scores that exceed 21), the pot carries over into the next game.

This game is easy to learn and easy to play but the real trick is being able to read your opponents and weigh up what sort of values they might have rolled.

Drinking Contest

What's a tavern without a good ol' drinking game? The aim is simple: to outlast your opponent in a test of intoxication. Each participant will roll a dice pool of 2d6 to determine how well you have handled your drink. The aim is for your total dice value to beat a score of five or more. Any less is counted as a wobble, five wobbles or three consecutive wobbles and you're on the floor and out of the game. At the end of three rounds, any players remaining upright must add a d4 to their dice pools. The d4 value is then subtracted from your 2d6 total each round. In subsequent rounds, additional d4's can be added and subtracted if certain conditions are met, however, all players after the third round must have at least one d4 in their dice pool. An additional d4 is added to a players dice pool every time the total score at the end of a round is equal to three or less. Players may subtract a d4 from their dice pool for rolling doubles on threes or higher. When this happens, that player also automatically succeeds the round. This continues until one remaining player is able to stand (figuratively speaking) victorious! Please roll responsibly.

Tolerance variant

Another way to play this game is to first set each player's tolerance. At the beginning of the game each player rolls 2d4. This value represents their tolerance level. The number they roll is the score they have to beat in order to avoid a wobble. So a player that rolls a two has a really high tolerance and is more difficult to beat than someone with a tolerance level of eight. However, even though a player with a tolerance of two may avoid a wobble by scoring two or more, after the third round rolling a value of three or less still results in the addition of another d4 to that player's dice pool.

Drinks and Daggers

There's nothing better than a bit of competition after a few rounds of drinks, especially when there's a bit of danger involved. Drinks and Daggers is a game played by two or more people, usually after a skin full. Some may possess a natural talent for this game while sober, but under the shroud of alcohol, it's a level playing field. Some brave proprietors may have a Drinks and Daggers board set up inside the taproom proper, whereas others may choose to have a designated area outside for this game. The aim of the game is to score the most points, and to get points participants throw daggers at a target. The target is usually painted with rings, the closer to the centre your dagger lands, the more points you get.

To play the game each player takes it in turns to roll 2d8. The table below corresponds to the outcome and accuracy of the throw. After five daggers, the scores are calculated and a winner is decided.

Sometimes mistakes can happen, and sometimes things happen that some would call skill and others would call a fluke. When you roll doubles on your turn it can either make you look really good or really bad, depending on whether you've hit the board or not. If you roll doubles on a miss consult the mishap table for the result, if you roll doubles on a hit consult the flourish table to see how you've impressed everyone.

Good luck to you and everyone that stands in the vicinity of the board while you play.

Dagger Throw 2d8

2	The dagger flies off in a random direction (mishap)
3	The blade just barely catches the target (1 point)
4	You inadvertently release the dagger on the backswing (mishap on a double)
5	The dagger tentatively lands in the outermost ring (1 point)
6	The dagger hits handle first (mishap on a double)
7	The dagger lands cleanly in the middle ring (2 points)
8	You send out the dagger in a chaotic spin, hitting everything but the target (mishap on a double)
9	You take a moment to finish your drink (roll again)
10	With a flick of the wrist the dagger flies into the target (2 points) (flourish on a double)
11	The dagger gets caught in your clothing, causing you to miss, miserably
12	That's how it's done, centre ring! (3 points) (flourish on a double)
13	Competitors and spectators flinch as the dagger heads for them and not the target
14	Was that a bullseye? Not quite but what a throw! (3 points) (flourish on a double)
15	You hit the target! Oh wait, no you didn't!
16	Bullseye! (5 points) (flourish)

Mishap d6

1	The dagger ricochets and lands in a surface near someone's head
2	If your intention was to smash as many things as possible, you're winning
3	You drop your drink and now you feel sad
4	Despite your efforts you lose balance and end up on the floor
5	Somehow you've managed to cut yourself
6	You were facing the wrong way!

Flourish d6

1	You threw the dagger while finishing your drink
2	You hit the target without looking
3	You show everyone that it was your offhand!
4	You take a bow, encouraging some spectators to start watching and cheering
5	It was so impressive that the barkeep hands you a drink on the house
6	You throw a second and it lands in the handle of the first, proving it wasn't a fluke

Tavern Generator

In this section, you will find a series of roll tables that will help you generate a tavern of your own. Use the tables to invent a name along with the services it has available, interesting features and secrets it might have and a bit of background.

Name Generator

d6 Format

1	The Adjective Title
2	The Noun & Noun
3	The Adjective Noun Title
4	The Adjective Noun
5	The Noun & Noun Title
6	The Title of Adjective Noun's

d4 Title

1	Bar
2	Tavern
3	Inn
4	Pub

d12 Noun

1	Goblin
2	Bandit
3	Horse
4	Wolf
5	Knight
6	Hammer
7	Crow
8	Tankard
9	Witch
10	Pirate
11	Warrior
12	Sword

d12 Adjective

1	Blushing
2	Brave
3	Clumsy
4	Sneaky
5	Cunning
6	Cheeky
7	Mighty
8	Hidden
9	Timid
10	Dull
11	Noble
12	Sleepy

Unique Feature - d12

1	Themed nights
2	Fighting pit in the centre
3	Bigger on the inside
4	Doesn't serve alcohol
5	It's also a brewery
6	No furniture
7	Holds nightly music competitions
8	Multiple areas for gambling
9	Pitch dark inside
10	Served by spectral waiters
11	No longer open for business
12	It's part of a chain

Services Available - d6
(roll up to four times)

1	Food
2	Rooms
3	Stabling
4	Blacksmith
5	Merchant
6	Bards/ Entertainment

Hidden Information - d8

1	Secret gang hideout
2	Hidden shrine for a cult
3	Guarding the entrance to a labyrinth
4	Hiding a criminal
5	Slave trade
6	Illegal goods trade
7	Underground fight club
8	Rebel base

Background - d8

1	Used to be a forge
2	Has never been popular
3	Used to be the theatre
4	Has changed hands many times
5	Used to belong to a famous adventurer
6	Has burned down four times!
7	Has been owned by the same family for generations
8	Has only just opened

Home Brew

Taverns, inns, ales and spirits, you have found all of these in the book so far. But the best is yet to come as we have included space in the back of this book for you to let your creative juices flow.

There is plenty of space for you to store details on your own taverns and NPCs!

Name: _____

Description

_____
_____
_____
_____
_____
_____
_____

A Bit 'O' History

_____
_____
_____
_____
_____
_____

Reviews

_____
_____
_____
_____
_____
_____
_____

Name: _____

Description

_____
_____
_____
_____
_____
_____
_____
_____
_____

A Bit 'O' History

_____
_____
_____
_____
_____
_____
_____

Reviews

_____
_____
_____
_____
_____
_____
_____
_____

Name: _____

Description

_____

_____

_____

_____

_____

_____

_____

A Bit 'O' History

_____

_____

_____

_____

_____

Reviews

_____

_____

_____

_____

_____

_____

Name: _____

Description

A Bit 'O' History

Reviews

Name:

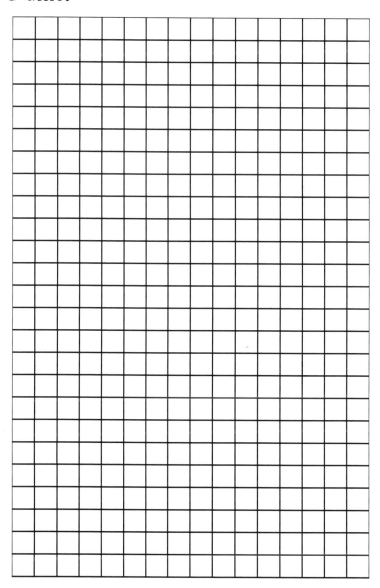

Points of Interest:

_____

_____

_____

_____

_____

_____

_____

_____

_____

_____

Notes:

_____

_____

_____

_____

_____

_____

_____

_____

Name:

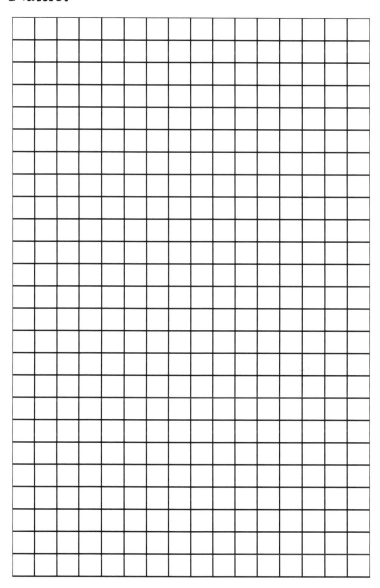

Points of Interest:

_____

_____

_____

_____

_____

_____

_____

_____

_____

_____

Notes:

_____

_____

_____

_____

_____

_____

_____

_____

Name:

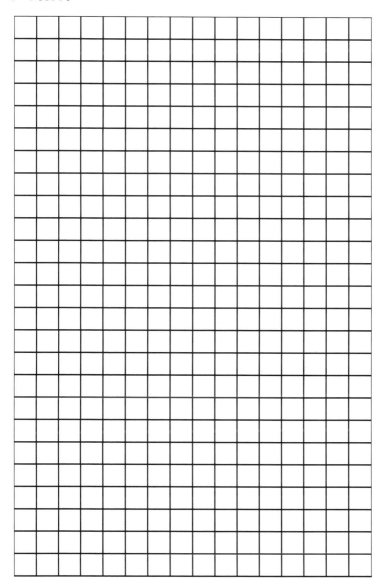

Points of Interest:

_____

_____

_____

_____

_____

_____

_____

_____

_____

_____

Notes:

_____

_____

_____

_____

_____

_____

_____

NPC notes
Name:
Race:
Job Role:
Description:

Likes:	Fears:
Dislikes:	Flaws:
Wants:	

NPC notes
Name:
Race:
Job Role:
Description:

Likes:	Fears:
Dislikes:	Flaws:
Wants:	

NPC notes
Name:
Race:
Job Role:
Description:

Likes:	Fears:
Dislikes:	Flaws:
Wants:	

NPC notes
Name:
Race:
Job Role:
Description:

Likes:	Fears:
Dislikes:	Flaws:
Wants:	

NPC notes
Name:
Race:
Job Role:
Description:

Likes:	Fears:
Dislikes:	Flaws:
Wants:	

NPC notes
Name:
Race:
Job Role:
Description:

Likes:	Fears:
Dislikes:	Flaws:
Wants:	

143

NPC notes
Name:
Race:
Job Role:
Description:

Likes:	Fears:
Dislikes:	Flaws:
Wants:	

NPC notes
Name:
Race:
Job Role:
Description:

Likes:	Fears:
Dislikes:	Flaws:
Wants:	

We would like to say a big thank you to all those who supported us throughout the project. It would not have been possible without you.

Thank you to the brilliant Justin Kemp of Biggs Studio who immersed himself in our fantasy worlds to design the beautiful illustrations that make the book what it is.

A final thanks to all the contributors that shared with us their stories, their taverns, and their characters that makes this project so unique.

Adam Francour
Amanda F.
Ammon Hope
Andrew Howard
Angela Wiwczor
Armin Huneburg
Ashley Harvey
Birne Gilmore
Bjorn Flintberg
Carl Harrison
Chris King
Curt L. Koenig
Danny C
Darcy Perry
David Ruskin
David Starkey
Doktor
Doug "Kosh" Williamson
Duckybank
Eugene Doherty
Finn

Florian Becke
Florian Kastell
Frits Kuijlman
Gareth Jones
George Monnat, Jr.
Hurmly
Jake Olver
James Joubert
Jason K
Jason Trupkin
Jed Kornbluh
Jim McLaughlin
John "Lord Shadowcat" Ickes
John Vots
Joseph B. Prozinski
Joshua Flavell-Blizard
Lee Jagger
Luc Jaullen
Leigh Wood
Manny Payan
Mark Hunt

Michael and Sarah
Mitchell Ortuondo
Nate Hammer
Patrick J Strezihar
Patrick Rippeto
Rob McPherson
Sam "Bifford" & The Wiltshire White Horse RPG Group
Samual Vinci
Symatt
Tara Harvey
Teddy Lattimore
The Guardians
Theonlymad
Tim "Thoth" Cooke
Timothy Baker
Travis Washeck
Tyty Smith
Yexil
Yianni Charalambopoulos

Printed in Great Britain
by Amazon